THE TRAIL TO REVOLUTION

PLAINSMAN WESTERN SERIES BOOK FOUR

B.N. RUNDELL

WOLFPACK
PUBLISHING
— EST 2013 —

The Trail to Revolution
Print Edition
© Copyright 2022 B.N. Rundell

Wolfpack Publishing
5130 S. Fort Apache Rd. 215-380
Las Vegas, NV 89148

wolfpackpublishing.com

Paperback ISBN 978-1-63977-422-7
eBook ISBN 978-1-63977-421-0
LCCN 2021952673

The year is 2021 as I write this book. It has been a trying year for many, our household included. The dreaded plague of Covid visited us, and that was just the beginning. But through it all, our gracious Lord was present in the form of family that came from distant states to help, friends nearby that kept us in their prayers, and the unfailing promises in His Word. But ours is not the only home that had its challenges, for many had greater difficulties whether it be disease, injury, loss, or other hardships. So, it is without apology that I dedicate this to the one who never fails, Our Lord and Savior, Jesus Christ. May our gratitude never wane, our dependence never fail, and our love never diminish. Thank You.

THE TRAIL TO REVOLUTION

1 / MOUNTAINS

The granite peaks of the front range marched like a garrison of stiff-backed soldiers, keeping guard over all access to the towering Rocky Mountains that stretched beyond the limits of sight. Reuben Grundy and his wife, Elly, had been watching the mountains rise higher and higher for the last two days of their westward trek. What had been a jagged western horizon had begun to take the shape of the magnificent mountain peaks that stood gallantly lifting their grey heads against the azure blue of the cloudless sky. The lower climes were arrayed in deep blue/green, even black, timber that appeared as tufted kilts, each with its own patterned and colorful tartan spread wide to cover the foothills that carried the spring runoff in its folds. The aspen, scrub oak, and willows intermingling with the spruce, pines, and firs that blanketed the mountains giving the appearance of the Creator having an exceptional creative day of coloring his handiwork.

Reuben reined up, resting his forearms on the saddle horn and took in the panoramic vista that stretched north and south farther than he could see, looked at the blonde, blue-eyed smiling woman at his side, and chuckled, "I was just thinkin'. The same Creator that made that," waving his hand to take in the entire mountain range, "is the one that made you for me! That must have been his practice handiwork and then He fashioned you!"

Elly shook her head as she smiled at her husband of less than a year, giggled and asked, "Are you sure He didn't make you for me?"

"Well, whichever way it was, you're stuck with me now!"

"I wouldn't have it any other way!" she replied, standing in her stirrups for a better look at the wide valley floor that lay before the black timbered mountains. The plains, with the buffalo grass, prickly pear cacti, sage, and greasewood, gave way to a green bottom that straddled the headwaters of the South Platte River. Their trek of the past week and more had brought them from Julesburg, Colorado Territory, to the growing town of Denver City. They had made this trip before at the request of Ben Holladay, owner of the Overland Stage company and had been instrumental in preventing a band of Confederate guerrillas from stealing a shipment of gold that came from the goldfields of Colorado to the Union forces back east. But now they were on a journey of their own, wanting to see the west.

With the Rocky Mountains beckoning, they planned a brief stop in Denver to deposit some funds with the Clark, Gruber and Company, resupply, and continue their journey of discovery. Reuben, a broad shouldered six-foot blond clean-shaven man, rode a long-legged blue roan gelding that had served him well since shortly after the left Berdan's Sharpshooters, the Union Cavalry unit he joined shortly after the war started. Discharged because of his wounds, and after his brother died in his arms, he returned home to White Pigeon, Michigan, to find his family murdered by a renegade band calling themselves the Home Guard. After tracking them down and serving justice as a deputy sheriff, he continued west, had a brief run-in with some bushwhackers, Redlegs and Quantrill's raiders, then spent a winter at Fort Kearny. But not to be deterred from his western quest, he met Eleanor Mae McGuire, who was traveling with her family on a Mormon wagon train. She was a pretty blonde that barely made five feet, with a trim figure and cheerful countenance that betrayed her confident and strong manner and was a woman that was more skilled with her Henry repeater than she was with a skillet, but willing to use both as necessary.

They were married soon after, and she now rode a soft-eyed leopard Appaloosa mare given her by Little Raven's Arapaho wives as a wedding present. Elly was outfitted with a .36 caliber Colt Pocket pistol in a holster on her left hip, butt forward, her .44 caliber Henry repeater rifle, and a Flemish knife kept in a sheath that hung between her shoulder blades.

Reuben had served as a Sharpshooter, using his skill with a Sharps rifle and side mounted telescope, and was credited with helping the 1st Sharpshooters gain the success and notoriety that had established their reputation as a unit that would often turn the tide of a battle to their favor. He had added a Spencer repeater, a Henry lever action repeater, and a Remington Army revolver to his arsenal, together with his favored Bowie knife and metal tomahawk that always were a part of his normal attire.

With a well-loaded pack mule trailing behind, free

rein, he nudged his roan off the slight rise to cross the meandering South Platte River to make their way to the Planter's House on the corner of Sixteenth and Blake Streets. They had stayed there on their last trip as the station for the Overland Stage occupied a part of the building, and the bank was just around the corner.

Denver City was a bustling town, rebuilding after a fire that almost destroyed the entire downtown, but the Pikes Peak Gold rush was still drawing families and prospectors from all points east, many just wanting to get away from the war that was still being waged in the east, especially after President Lincoln had issued the Emancipation Proclamation that freed all the slaves. A war that many thought would be over in a few months, was now going into its third year with no end in sight.

Although Colorado territory had not been actively engaged in the war, no battles were fought in the territory thus far, it was rife with conflict with many Southern Sympathizers showing their colors and flying the stars and bars whenever an opportunity was given. But the Unionists were in the majority and units had been recruited to join the fight in the east. Reuben was well aware of the conflict, having encountered a Confederate Guerilla band that tried to steal the gold shipment he had sworn to protect. Those were the memories that flooded his consciousness as he stepped down to tether his mount at the hitchrail in front of the Planter's House.

He gave Elly his hand to help her down, knowing it was a stretch for such a small woman, but it was the mannerly thing to do, regardless. Elly dusted herself off as she stepped up to the boardwalk and smiled at her man as he joined her. As soon as they stepped through the double doors of the hotel, they were greeted by the clerk with a "Welcome Folks!" The clerk was a young man with a white linen shirt, a starched collar, sleeve garters and a brocade vest that threatened to pop its buttons as it fought to cover the rotund figure. His broad smile split his ruddy complexioned face and his thicket of curly hair fell over his black single brow that shaded his little eyes that sat above round pink cheeks.

Reuben smiled, "Howdy! Need a room for the night."

"We've got one room left. You are in luck, sir!"

Elly stepped beside Reuben, looking at the young man, "And could you have a bath readied for me please?"

"Certainly, ma'am. The bathroom is just down the hall from your room, and I'll have the maid ready if for you right away," he answered, holding the quill pen out for Reuben to sign the register.

The clerk looked at the name, "Mr. and Mrs. Grundy, you are most welcome. Here is the key to your room and if you like, I'll have someone help you with your luggage."

"That won't be necessary. I'll take care of it," answered Reuben, turning to Elly. He handed her the key, nodded, and turned back to get their gear. He soon returned with bedrolls and saddle bags, went to the room, and pushed the door open with his foot. Elly was standing at the window, looking at the view of the edge of town and the mountains in the distance. Reuben walked up behind her, put his arms around her waist and his chin on her shoulder. "You have your bath. I'll take the animals to the livery at the stage station, then I'll go to the bank. I'll be back shortly, but you can tell the maid to have a bath waiting for me, if you will."

Elly twisted around to look at her man with a big smile. "Oh, you know I will!" and giggled as he held her close. She pushed him back, held her nose with her fingers, and said, "Tend to the horses! You're beginning to smell just like 'em!"

"After two weeks in the saddle, you ain't no lily patch, girl!" replied Reuben, laughing. He turned away as she, giggling, slapped at his arm. He feigned hurt, grinned, and slipped out the door to disappear down the hallway.

2 / FRIENDS

E lly chose to disrobe in the room with the bath, having no extra robe for traversing the hall, and dropped her clothes in a heap beside the deep copper tub, placing her knife and sheath and her pistol and holster on the small table that held the lye soap and dish. Clean tepid water invited and a knock at the door announced the arrival of a maid with a pot of hot water. "Pardon me, ma'am," stated the woman with the copper pot swinging at her side as she approached the tub. Elly held her jacket before her as she watched the chambermaid pour the steaming water into the tub, causing a rise of bubbles to surface and bringing a smile to Elly's face. She looked at the woman, her floor length dark-blue homespun dress covered with a white linen apron, and smiled. "Thank you, that looks very inviting."

The maid nodded, "Give it a try and if you need more water, I'll fetch it rightway!"

Elly stepped close, tested the water with her toes and nodded, "It feels just fine!" and dropped her jacket atop the other clothes, and stepped into the copper tub with the rolled edge and high back. The chambermaid lay a

7

pair of towels atop her weapons on the side table, handed Elly a washcloth and a long-handled brush, "Will that be all, ma'am? Or would you like me to scrub your back?"

"Would you? That would be nice," answered Elly, leaning forward to offer her back to the maid. The woman picked up the brush, dipped it in the water and lathered it with the bar soap and began to scrub Elly's back. A ruckus outside the door caught their attention as some bellowing and sputtering accompanied a thump on the wall and clod hoppers stomping on the floor. Suddenly a loud thud knocked on the door, the door jamb splintered, and a big drunken sot staggered through the door, caught his balance, and looked through bleary eyes at the two women. The chambermaid had her back to the door, her body shielding Elly, and she turned, brush raised as she shouted, "Here! Here! Remove yourself at once!"

"Eh? Whadda we got here?" grumbled the man as he staggered to one side, trying to see past the enraged maid. "What'chu gonna do wit' that brush? Think you can spank me like my momma usta?" His words were slurred, his stature stumbling, and his eyesight obviously blurred as he raised his eyebrows high to open his eyes wide. "Wal! Ya got room in there fer another'n, missy? Hehehe!" he asked as he stumbled to one side trying to see into the tub, caught his balance and started unbuttoning his shirt.

Elly had slipped her hand under the towels and retrieved her Colt pocket pistol and peered around the chambermaid, glaring at the big drunk, "No, but if you don't hightail it outta here, you're gonna find yourself a little heavier with some lead in your britches!" She was leaning forward, and only her head and the pistol were visible to the inebriated beast.

"Ah, you ain't gonna shoot me! Not with that toy! It ain't even a real pistol. You just hold on there, I'll be with you real quick like!"

"Last warning! Leave or I'll shoot!" declared Elly.

"Hah!" declared the man, starting to strip his shirt.

The pistol roared and bucked, rattling the window-panes beside the tub. The bullet went true and struck exactly where Elly aimed, practically nailing the man's foot to the floor. She cocked the pistol again, readying a second shot and lifted the muzzle to aim at the man's head. The big man screamed, blubbered, and began dancing on one foot, grabbing the bleeding foot with both hands. "YOU SHOT ME! You . . . you . . . YOU SHOT ME!"

"Next one will be between your eyes!" she warned.

The maid had dropped the brush, put both hands to her mouth, eyes wide and glaring as she stood frozen in place, watching the big man whimper and lean against the opened door, tears coming to his eyes. She began to chuckle, looked down at the little woman in the tub that held the pistol, unwavering and tried to stifle her laugh but failed.

The big man's eyes flared, and he dropped his wounded foot to the floor, roared as he started to move toward the tub, but Reuben appeared in the doorway, "What's goin' on!" he demanded.

"That man tried to get in the tub with m'lady!" shouted the chambermaid, pointing at the rogue that limped as he turned toward the new threat.

Reuben's eyes flared as he grabbed the big man by the scruff of his neck, spinning him around and pushing him out the door of the bathroom. The chambermaid leaned to the side to see into the hall, but turned to look at Elly, "He your man?"

"Ummhmm," replied Elly, reaching for the dropped washcloth, apparently unconcerned.

But the sounds came from the hall of retreating boots, the muffled complaints of the big man, and the sound of a door slammed open. The fading scream of someone falling was ended by the banging of a door closing, and more footsteps became louder as they neared the door. Reuben stuck his head in, "You alright?"

"Ummhmm. I'll be done soon, then you can have at it!"

"He won't be back. He decided to take his bath in the horse trough below the steps out yonder. I'm not sure if he can swim, but he sure was tryin'!" He chuckled and reached for the door to shut off the bathroom and give his wife her privacy.

THE HANDSOME COUPLE CAUGHT THE EYE OF EVERYONE IN the dining room as they entered to find a table and take a meal. Reuben escorted Elly to the familiar table beside the window overlooking 16th Street and pulled the chair out for her. She flashed him a smile and took her seat, her black split skirt flaring to cover the chair, the fringe on the sleeves of the leather jacket draping over the arms of the chair and her blonde tresses hanging down her back in three loose braids.

Reuben took his chair opposite her, setting his flat brimmed black hat on the chair beside the window, and undoing the buttons on his black leather fringed jacket that was similar to Elly's, both made from ram skins by the same craftsman. His black corded britches were tucked into his high-topped boots, and his white linen shirt was adorned by a loose string tie.

They were no sooner seated than a shout came from the door and a pair of whiskery old-timers, grinning ear to ear came stumbling toward them. "Reuben! Elly! Wal, ain'tchu a sight fer sore eyes!" declared Windy, tugging at Whip's sleeve to hurry him along. "Say, you got room fer two more?" he asked, motioning to the empty chairs.

"For you two? Of course!" answered Reuben, standing to greet their friends from the stage line. Whip was a driver, Windy his shotgunner, and they met when Reuben and Elly were working for Ben Holladay, the owner of the stage line.

As the two men were seated, a quick glance took in their familiar attire, Windy in his buckskins and whiskers, Whip in his corded britches and linsey Woolsey shirt, all held together by his galluses. The two men had been partners on the stage line for a couple years and many trips on the Platte River trail, also known as the Overland Trail between Julesburg and Denver City. Windy, always the more talkative of the two was showing his less than perfect teeth with a wide grin as he looked from Reuben to Elly, and a quick glance around the room and lowering his voice, "You two still working as undercover deputy marshals?"

Reuben chuckled. "Well, we tried to turn in the badges, but Holladay wouldn't hear of it, and he said the governor wasn't wantin' us to give 'em up either. But we told him we weren't interested, not that it did any good. But as far as we're concerned, well, he said we should check in by telegram, but you know, we just haven't seen one o' them there telegrams!"

The two old-timers chuckled, looking from Reuben to Elly and Elly added, "Plus, we just wanted some time to ourselves. We thought we'd head for the mountains, maybe find a place for a cabin, just enjoy some time together!" She reached for Reuben's hand and clasped it as she smiled at him.

"Well, after what'chu two done about that gold shipment and discouraging those Rebels, we ain't had no trouble from them fer a while. But we been hearing some o' them short lines in the gold field country have had a few hold-ups, but nothing whut says they're Southern sympathizers."

Windy started to say more but was interrupted when a waitress came to their table to take their orders after giving each a cup of steaming coffee. She smiled and winked at Windy, "So, short-stuff, what'chu gonna have tonight?"

Windy grunted, frowned and looked at the waitress, a rather buxom woman of middle-age and a bit portly, "Now, Miss Ethel, is that any way to talk to your best customer? And I might add your best-looking customer?" chuckling as he leaned back and lay his arms over the back of the chair, smiling at the woman.

She giggled a little, then pointed to a table near the corner. "You see that man in the dark jacket sitting at that table yonder?"

"Ummhmm, shore do, why?"

"Cuz he's what'chu call a optom . . . uh . . . eye doctor. And he could get you a pair of them newfangled spectacles so you could see what I see when I look at you! Might change your story! Now, what'chu gonna have, short-stuff." She grinned at Windy, knowing he did not like the nickname, but she was half a head taller and delighted in ribbing the man.

Windy looked around the table at the others, got a

nod from each one, and looked back at Miss Ethel and said, "Specials all around!"

"Coming up!" she declared, giving Windy another wink as she turned away.

Elly laughed. "I think she has her cap set for you, Windy, are you thinking about settling down?"

"Me? Hah! I'm too young and too handsome to settle down! I've got too much living left to do!" he chuckled as he twisted around in his chair to reach for his coffee.

3 / FOOTHILLS

"Wal, I'm purty certain they ain't give up, but I don't reckon there's another bunch of 'em like we run into before. What with them getting the whipping what was dealt to 'em by our boys in blue. But there's allus gonna be some what acts like they's doing it fer the Confederacy, but they just rob whoever an' whatever an' keep it their ownselves," declared Windy, leaning on the top rail of the stall where Reuben was saddling his blue roan.

"Has there been much trouble since that last go 'round?" asked Reuben, tightening the girth and checking the gear. Behind the cantle, his bedroll sat atop the saddle bags, and on the far side the scabbard that carried the Sharps hung beneath the right stirrup fender. He had carried the Henry in a similar scabbard on the left side, but recently chose to put it together with the Spencer atop the panniers on the pack mule. A haversack, that carried some of his extra clothing and other accouterments, was secured atop and behind the bedroll.

Whip stood beside Windy and added, "But there's been some talk that those stage lines what run in the goldfields have been gettin' held up, usually when the word gets out they're carryin' dust an' such."

"Are there really that many people an' towns that they've got their own stage lines?" asked Elly, rigging her Appaloosa in the next stall.

"Wal, there ain't there so many now as what they was when the rush first started. What with the war going on an' such, but what sent a lot of 'em packing was the winters! Why, up thar in South Park the snow gets nigh onto twenty feet deep, and the wind blows all the time, sounds like a screaming banshee it do!" explained Windy. "But there's still a lot o' folks a digging an' grubbing fer gold. But the ones making the most money is them comp'nys building the roads. What with freight wagons, stage lines, gold-seekers, an' more, the gov'ner done let a bunch o' contracts to build roads ever which way. An' once they got 'em built, they make 'em toll roads an' charge ever'body!"

"You don't say," said Reuben, turning to look at the pair.

"I do indeed!"

"So, if we were to want to go up there just to see what's goin' on, which way would you recommend?" asked Reuben, backing Blue out of the stall.

The two men stepped aside and looked at one another. Whip answered with, "Where you wanna be is on the North Fork of the South Platte. You *could* take the Turkey Creek Road if you wanna pay a toll, or you could just take the trail up Deer Creek, it'll cross over, take you south a ways, then you'll hit the North Fork. It sides a long mountain ridge topped off by twin cone peaks at the west end. You'll round that end, and you can foller the road o'er Kenosha Pass an' drop down into the upper end of South Park."

"How far?" asked Elly, backing the appy out of her stall.

"Oh, two, three days, dependin'," answered Whip. "Lot o' purty country up there in them mountains, you might just wanna take yore time and have a good look-see!" he chuckled.

"You boys headed out on a run this morning?" asked Elly, walking her appy to the big door of the Stage Line livery. The men had walked beside her, leaving Reuben to finish rigging the mule and coming along behind.

"Yes'm, reckon we'll be spending the night in Latham. Long day, but it ain't a bad run, longs we don't run into any brigands," answered Windy, shaking his head, "'Course I got muh shotgun handy!"

"Well, you two take it easy, an' maybe we'll be back this way and you can buy us supper!" she smiled and leaned over to kiss each one of the men on the cheek.

Windy sputtered and dropped his eyes as he wiped his cheek, stubbing his toe in the dirt but the voice of Reuben caught his attention.

"Hey you two! What'chu doin' kissin' on my wife!" he kidded, laughing at the embarrassed duo.

"We was just sayin' goodbye!" declared Whip, looking at Reuben with a sidelong glance, knowing the man was joshing.

Reuben and Elly stepped aboard their horses and nudged them out the big door of the livery, the first light of early morning chasing away the shadows. The livery faced the north, and the sunlight was on their right shoulders until they turned down 16th and put it at their backs. They twisted around in their saddles and waved to their friends, anxious to put the city behind them, for even at this early hour, the streets and roads were showing a lot of activity. At the south edge of town, they soon came to the Platte, followed it a short way to the west and came to Deer Creek, the small stream that came from the mountains on a southeasterly route and would show them the way into the mountains.

They stayed on the north side of the river, following the narrow Deer Creek that pointed toward the foothills that rose in the distance. Before them a long hogback ridge rose like a barrier to the hills, but the 'v' notch cut by the creek also sided a trail on the north edge. The hogback, though barren on the lower levels, held a grey freckled canopy of twisted piñon, scrub oak, and sage that shadowed the rocky crest that looked like the off side of a wilted rooster's comb. The green creek bottom held chokecherry, willows and boxelder with random cottonwood and occasional aspen standing tall. Once through the notch of the hogback, another little brother hogback paralleled the larger one but showed itself to be more rumpled and rockier.

Another notch put them through the smaller ridge and into the red dirt and rocks common in the area. The pale pink color of the big slab rock often faced the entire hillside, showing slanted layers of the soft rock that was often interspersed with stunted juniper brush showing the contrasting green between the slabs of pale pink and white.

Deer Creek pointed them west into the mountains as the foothills pushed into the little stream, making it twist its way out of the higher climes. The trail hugged the creek and the farther they pushed into the hills, the greener the slopes showed with Spruce and Fir trees clinging to the north facing slopes, leaving the south slopes to show green with grasses and outcroppings of granite and limestone. They had traversed about six or seven miles when Reuben remembered Whip saying,

"After you've ridden, oh, six, seven miles, you'll come to a bit of a crook in the trail. You can either go north or south, north will take you on an easy trail that will join the road from Turkey Creek. If'n I was you, that's the way I'd go."

He turned to look at Elly who was obviously enjoying the scenery, looking at all the wildflowers and the rising hills, "Reckon we'll turn north a spell. You wanna step down and stretch your legs, or keep goin'?"

"Oh, I'll wait till we need to stop for nooning!" She smiled, nodding for him to keep moving. They left the Deer Creek trail and followed the faint trail that had been either an ancient trail of the natives, or a well-used game trail. It twisted through the trees and stayed in the bottom of the draw, the sandy bottom telling of spring runoffs that had carved its way to the bigger creeks. Blue Spruce, Fir, Ponderosa Pine and scattered maple and alder, interspersed with juniper and random clusters of aspens, fought for footing on the steep hillsides that rose on either side, and still the south facing slopes appeared bald save for the variety of grasses, bunch grass, Indian grass, gramma and more.

Mule deer had been plentiful along the creek bed, many coming for their morning water and the moist grasses by the stream, but now they were in the hills that offered shelter but little water. Elly spotted a coyote that prompted the pup, Bear, to rise from his seat on her bedroll and growl, but Elly said, "Easy, Bear, you go after him, and you'll have to walk the rest of the way!" She had her arm around his neck and spoke firmly to the growing pup. He seemed to be growing faster than the weeds beside the trail, his big paws filling Elly's palms, his head almost as big as hers and his thick fur making him appear even bigger. He had been a recent addition to their number, found along the trail at what had been an overnight campsite of wagon trains and probably left behind by someone that had more than they could handle. He showed all the signs of becoming a big dog and his resemblance to a wolf made Reuben suspect he was the product of a wildlife mating along the trail.

The trail had turned north, and the hills appeared to lay back away from the gulch. The hills on both sides showed an abundance of juniper and piñon. Dust rose ahead telling Reuben they were nearing the Turkey Creek road. A bit of brighter green showed in a draw to their right and Reuben nodded toward the cut and pointed Blue into the draw. The tall cottonwoods promised some water and a small spring trickled from the rocks to feed a shallow pool about double the size of a big frying pan.

They stepped down and Elly let the pup run free to investigate the new surroundings. "Go ahead and get you a drink 'fore Bear muddies everythin' up!" suggested Reuben, loosening the girth on his saddle. Elly bellied down by the pool and took a deep drink of the cold fresh water, wiped her face as she sat up, and looking to Reuben, "Good water! Better get your drink before the horses!"

The animals were ground tied, but they also smelled the water and Reuben had to push Blue aside to get his drink. He went to one knee, scooped water in his palm and surrendered the little pool to Blue and the Appy, who were soon pushed aside by the mule. Elly had fetched a pouch of pemmican and shared some with Reuben as they seated themselves in the shade of cotton-wood. Reuben pointed to the side of the tree, "Look there," and Elly's eyes grew large as she asked, "Bear?"

"Ummhmm, same as we got back east, black bear.

19

And that was prob'ly made this mornin' when he came here for water. Or maybe that was a female. There's some cub tracks yonder, see?" as he pointed to a miniature version of the nearer tracks. "They say there's grizzly in these mountains and they're a lot bigger and meaner than the black bear. Their tracks are a bit different, bigger, and longer claws."

"How much bigger?" asked Elly, not sure she wanted to hear the answer.

"Oh, prob'ly twice as big!" chuckled Reuben.

She patted the pistol at her hip. "Would this stop him?"

"Nope. Just make him mad."

She shook her head, tore off a piece of pemmican, and chewed like she was mad.

With just a short break to give the horses a breather and drink from the little spring, Reuben and Elly were soon back on the trail. As soon as they accessed the roadway, they rode side by side, the mule trailing behind the roan. Because Blue and the mule were long-time trail companions, Reuben often let the mule follow free-rein and he would usually take advantage of any trail or road that allowed him to be beside the roan, rather than follow-after.

The terrain was common for high foothills, north facing slopes thick with fir, spruce, and pine, south facing slopes bearing thickets of deep grass with scattered piñon and juniper among the big rocks and outcroppings. It was a pleasant country, peaceful with many birds giving forth their song, a favorite of Elly's being that of the yellow breasted meadowlark. She spotted a golden eagle circling high overhead and pointed him out to Reuben, "Oh, isn't he beautiful, he just floats on the wind." She heard the high-pitched scream and watched as he circled, then he tucked his wings and seemed to drop out of the sky like a rock until he neared the ground and his talons showed, wings spread, just as he caught a prairie dog running for his den, but the fat little hole-digger was too slow and in one smooth motion was taken from the ground, talons sunk deep in his sides, as the big eagle lifted ever upward and disappeared over the tree tops. Elly sat silent, mesmerized by nature's lesson of survival, and looked at Reuben.

Reuben saw the wonder, hurt, and question in his wife's eyes, but there was nothing he could say that would change the way of the wilderness and slowly shook his head as he turned away. He nodded toward a patch of flowers, "There's some flowers you've not seen before." A wide bed of blue and white columbines stretched their blossoms to the sun as if strutting their stuff for the passersby. Elly looked at the flowers, letting a smile replace the sadness with an appreciation for the Creator that lent such beauty to this remote country. She let her eyes wander and pointed out another cluster of blooms, most a darker blue and smaller blossom clusters hanging their heads. "Those look like tiny chiming bells!" She laughed. "And look there," pointing to a patch of tall flowers with long stalks that held an abundance of blooms, "those look like sweet peas, but I think they're called Lupine!"

The timber covered hills rose on either side of the roadway until the trail bent to the south and a wide park opened on the west edge of the road, rising halfway up the slope of the hill until the dark skirt of timber lay heavy on the mountain. As they entered from the north, movement near the tree line on the edge of the park caught their attention and Reuben reined up and nodded for Elly to look. A herd of elk, mostly cows and calves and a few yearlings, grazed on the upper reaches of the park, staying near the timber where they could easily escape if necessary.

"Ain't never seen a herd like that back home," stated Reuben, crossing his arms on the pommel of his saddle.

Elly looked at the multi-colored animals with their dark necks, chests and bellies, light brown sides and back, and pale rumps. "Look at the little ones! They're running and playing just like youngsters of all kinds." She laughed as she watched and was startled when Bear jumped up, put his front paws on her shoulders, and looked over her shoulder at the herd. She laughed again, patting the dog's paws. "Bear, what do you think you're doing?"

"Prob'ly showin' you who's the real boss!" chuckled Reuben, looking at the pair.

The elk were about three to four hundred yards away and showed little concern for the intruders below, as Reuben nudged Blue forward to start them back on the trail. After a mile, the roadway bent around a big rocky knob that held piñon, cedar, and juniper, all with tenuous footholds in the limestone cracks. The trail turned back to the west, surmounting the parallel ridges until they broke into another, much larger park that straddled the roadway. The bottom of the park carried a meandering, willow-lined stream that caught the runoff from the black timber covered mountain on the south edge and the rocky knolls to the north. The deep grass showed sign of many animals and the rocky knolls sprouted prospect holes with their yellow dirt diggings scarring the hillsides.

Reuben pushed through the willows beside the creek, found a nice clearing and stepped down. With a glance to Elly, "Good place for a noonin', ya reckon?"

She smiled, nodded, and pushed the pup to jump

down, then swung her leg over the cantle and belly slid down the fender of the saddle to reach the ground. After the horses had their drink, Reuben busied himself with stripping the gear and giving them a quick rubdown with handfuls of grass, then picketed them at the edge of the willows to let them graze. Elly had started a small fire and had a pot of water on for coffee and had some leftover frybread together with some thin slices of timpsila and smoked meat in a pan at the edge of the fire.

Reuben stood near the fire, stretched, and looked up the long grassy slope toward the tree line. Something moved and he watched as several cow elk with calves at their side strolled from the trees, made a quick survey of the area, and moved into the deep grass. The park was covered with tall Indian grass, some buffalo grass and gramma, all enticing and nourishing for the elk. The spindly-legged orange-colored calves stayed close to their mothers, until they grew bored and began to romp and play with one another.

"Ohoh," declared Reuben, quietly as he turned to the stack of gear and fetched his Sharps rifle. Elly watched him and when he returned to the side of the little fire, she looked where he nodded as he attached the side mounted scope to the rifle. He lifted the weapon to his shoulder and watched a big grizzly show himself at the edge of the trees. The bear stood, stretching to his full height to look at the elk and the calves.

Every bunch of elk usually has a mature cow that could be called the boss cow as she chooses the trails, the graze, watering, and watches over the herd. A big cow moved to the edge of the small herd, putting herself between them and the bear, watching the beast as he looked them over. When a couple calves wandered from the herd, romping at the lower edge in the deep grass, the bear came down to all fours and started moving toward the calves. The big cow spun around and squealed her warning, prompting the herd to move toward the trees. The big cow appeared to be driving the herd, pushing a laggard with her chest, but the two calves were slow in coming. Their mothers made the squeal of alarm, calling their calves and taking several hops toward them.

Elly spotted the big bear starting to lumber up to a run, his big back humping, and head low and he bounded toward the gangly calves. Elly gave a quick glance to Reuben. "Do something! He's gonna get the babies!"

Reuben looked at his woman, shaking his head. "Just what do you think I should do?" He held the rifle to his shoulder and watched the bear through the scope. He moved the rifle to his right to get a look at the fleeing herd and the calves, then swung back to the bear. The big bruin was gaining on the scrambling calves and two cows were moving toward them. It was not uncommon for the cows to try to defend their calves, even against a big bear. Reuben spotted a small outcropping of rocks between the bear and his prey, sighted in on the rocks and waited an instant until the bear neared, then squeezed off his shot. The rifle roared and belched smoke and lead, sending the bullet on its way. It splatted against the rocks, the bulk of the conical lead ricocheting away with a whine that could be heard at the camp. The bear stumbled, paused, and looked around for the cause of the interfering noise and more. He rose up on his hind legs, looking around, and with a glance at the disappearing herd and the calves, he looked to the bottom of the valley and the tethered horses.

Dropping to all fours, the bear started down the slope

toward his new prey. Reuben lowered the rifle, throwing open the lever and breech to reload. "Get the animals away!" he ordered as he slammed the lever back, driving the copper cartridge into the chamber. He lifted the rifle to his shoulder as Elly ran to the horses and mule, grabbed their leads, and pulled her appaloosa mare near a big rock, and stepped to the rock to swing aboard her horse. She had no sooner landed on its back and the horses got a whiff of the bear and turned their heads to see the brown beast lumbering down the slope. Elly dug her heels to the mare, jerked the leads of the roan and mule taut and took off across the road and up the opposite slope toward the trees.

The big Sharps bucked and roared again, this time the warning shot was between the front feet of the bear and the shock of the blast, the plume of smoke, and the smell of burnt gunpowder, gave the bear pause and he slid to a stop, stood again and with jaw snapping, he cocked his head to the side, pawed at the air with his massive paws and fearsome claws, he gave out a roar that seemed to make the grass bow down before him and the willows to wilt beside Reuben.

Another cartridge found its way into the breech and chamber, the breech closed and lever snapped, as Reuben lifted the rifle again, taking aim at the tuft of fur at the base of the monster of the mountain's throat, put his finger lightly on the thin front trigger and took a breath, let some out and began his draw, but stopped when the bear dropped to all fours, gave another growl and turned away to casually walk up the hillside with one backward glance over his shoulder, and disappear in the black timber.

Reuben kept the scope on the place where the bear entered the trees, and a moment later, satisfied he was gone, dropped to the ground, arched his back, and stretched as he lowered the hammer on the rifle. He held his hand out to see it tremble, took a deep breath to calm himself and slowly stood to look around for his woman and the horses. He saw her sitting astride her mare just below the tree line on the far side of the park, the furthest point in the big meadow away from the scene of the bear. Reuben waved her back and she started down the slope toward him. With another quick look at the place where the grizzly entered the trees, he sat the rifle down on the stack of gear and moved the pan of food and the coffee pot away from the fire. He smiled as Elly rode into the clearing and slid to the ground.

"Was that what you were thinkin' when you told me to do somethin'?" He chuckled.

She looked at him, shook her head, smiled, and slapped his arm. "Oh you!"

5 / STAGE

The crack of the bullwhip, shouts of the Jehu, and the rattle of trace chains announced the coming of the stage. The newly-built roadway had already carried a lot of traffic; freighters, gold seekers, and two different stage companies. Since the discovery of gold in the greater South Park region, the Pikes Peak Gold rush had been a magnet for fortune hunters of all types, from the prospectors to the tavern builders, from the women of the night to the claim jumpers and outlaws, and with a mix of would-be soldiers of both the blue and the grey, it held a hodge-podge of humanity. The stage companies were just another venture of fortune hunters.

As the stage drew near, Reuben and Elly moved away from the road, wanting neither a confrontation with the driver and his messenger, nor a dust bath from the passing. The six-up team leaned into their collars, traces taut, for it was a steady climb, although not a hard one, for the easy grade made a slow rise to the top of Kenosha pass at an elevation of about ten thousand feet, but that was still several miles away and the team would be changed at least twice before mounting the crest of the pass.

The driver cracked his whip over the heads of the horses, shouted his encouragement and lifted his head at the pair sitting horseback off the trail. It was a common occurrence to pass travelers on this road, whether in their wagons, horseback or afoot and he paid little attention to this pair, but something caught his attention, and he did a double take. He elbowed his shotgunner, "That was a woman!"

The shotgunner twisted in his seat for another look and turned back, "Danged if you ain't right! A good lookin' one too!" he shook his head and added, "I'd hate to see that blonde hair hangin' from some Injun's coup stick!"

"Maybe her man can protect her! 'Course some o' them miners ain't much better!"

Reuben looked at the stage and read *Kehler and Montgomery Stage Line* painted across the top above the door and windows. The curtains at each of the windows were drawn down in a futile effort to keep out the dust, while even the two passengers up top had handkerchiefs over their mouths. It had been several days since the last bit of rain and would probably be several more, making the fine dust on the roadway lift into a brown cloud to later filter down and cover what little greenery grew near the road.

Elly waved the dust away from her face, squinting her eyes as it passed, coughed, and said, "Oh, I am so glad we're not on a stage!" She lifted her neckerchief to cover her mouth and nose and nudged the appaloosa to the side of Blue. As the stage disappeared around a distant bend, the two travelers reveled in the quiet and beauty of the valley that lay at the foot of the long timber-covered ridge. It was but a little shy of three miles farther that the low-roofed log building that sat before a larger lean-to barn and big corrals that they spotted the stage coach. It was at a swing station stop and the passengers had scrambled from the dusty coach to knock some dust off, get a drink and make a quick trip to the outhouse before the messenger blew his trumpet to bid them board. The driver lifted his whip shoulder high, saw the two riders nearing the station and waited as they neared, "You folks goin' to South Park?" he asked as he leaned over the box.

"Maybe. Depends on which way the wind's blowin'!" answered Reuben, smiling.

"So, you're not lookin' for gold?" asked the driver.

"Just explorin' the country!" explained Reuben.

"Wal, keep an eye out! There's stories about some Ute Injuns causin' trouble!"

"Thank you, sir! We'll do that! You do the same!" replied Reuben, lifting his hand in a wave as the whip cracked and the fresh team leaned into their collars. The hostler stood against the fence; his work finished for the day as there would be no more stages through until tomorrow.

"How far to the next station?" asked Reuben, leaning on the pommel with arms crossed.

"Oh, 'bout thirteen, fourteen mile," drawled the hostler, a tall lean man with high-water britches held up with tied together galluses and showing his bare ankles above high-topped brogans. He reached to his mouth to remove a long sprig of hay, grinning at Reuben, and looking with a wry eye to Elly. "'Course, you could put up here. Only place we got is in the barn, but the hay mow can be right comf'tble," he added as he grinned at Elly.

Elly caught the man's leer and pushed her appy between Blue and the mule to put Reuben between her and the hostler. She whispered, "Let's get outta here! He gives me the heeby-jeebs!"

Reuben glanced sideways at Elly, nodded to the hostler, "Thanks!" and put his heels to the Blue to move away from the swing station and the hostler. He turned to his wife, "Heeby-jeebs?"

She shrugged and shivered, "Well, if he had looked at you the same way, you'd have blacked both his eyes!"

They had ridden no more than five miles when they overtook a man walking down the middle of the road, a haversack and bedroll over his shoulders. As they neared the man, he turned to watch them draw close and with a broad smile he greeted them, "Afternoon folks! Pleased to see fellow travelers on the road of life!" He stepped closer, extending his hand up toward Reuben, "I'm John Dyer, I'm an itinerant preacher with the Methodist Episcopal church, and I'm bound for South Park."

Reuben reined up and stepped down, reaching for the man's hand. "Pleased to meet you, Preacher. I'm Reuben Grundy, and this is my wife, Elly. We are also headed for South Park, although not necessarily by the shortest way. We're sort of wanderin' and explorin'."

"Oh? Looking for gold, are you?"

"No, no. We're just new to the mountains and are enjoyin' seein' God's creation."

"Well, bless you brother. It's good to meet someone that is more interested in what God has done than what he can take from the land." He turned away and resumed his walk, but kept talking to include the two new acquaintances, prompting Reuben to walk along with him, leading his roan and the mule trailing. Elly had moved the Appaloosa alongside the itinerant and leaned forward, listening to the men's conversation.

31

"So, where did you call home before you began wandering?" asked the preacher.

"Grew up in Michigan territory, went to war, lost my family and headed west. God was in it though, for that's how I met my wife, earlier this year."

"Oh, so you're newlyweds then?"

"Ummhmm."

"Well, congratulations and may the Lord abundantly bless your union! I had the good fortune of a happy marriage, fourteen years we were together and blessed with five children before she went on to glory without me." He grew silent, his eyes looking to the distance but his pace never wavering, until he turned to look at Reuben. "Here, here. Step aboard your fine mount, I can keep pace with you. You need not walk on my account."

Reuben nodded, drew Blue alongside and stepped aboard. The preacher walked between them and kept up his conversation, talking about his years on his circuit in South Park, Oro City, and Gunnison country.

"Folks say the winters in the Park are formidable; is that so?" asked Elly.

The preacher looked to her, smiling. "That depends on what you call formidable. Last winter I carried the mail from Tarryall and Fairplay over Mosquito pass to Oro City. I fashioned some skis like they use in Norway and made it alright. It does get a bit cold, thirty to fifty below zero, and the snow, well, the most I've seen has been taller than most houses, maybe twenty feet."

"Brrr," said Elly, her hands around her arms and shaking as if shivering in the cold, but her broad smile was warm.

The preacher and Reuben both chuckled until the preacher added, "But there are a lot of empty cabins that make for a warm abode in the winter. Several holes have played out or didn't pay enough for the men to winter in the mountains. Some were busy towns, but now nothing but empty holes, empty cabins, and shattered dreams."

"So, who do you preach to, then?" asked Elly.

The preacher stopped, rested his hand on the neck of the Appaloosa and smiled at Elly, "Whoever God puts in my way. There have been times that the crowds were more than a hundred, other times less than a handful. But every soul needs the Gospel, and they need to know the Savior!"

Elly smiled, glanced at Reuben, and looked down the road. They had kept to the road as it bent through a notch among the hills, then around a knob, and began to follow a willow-lined creek to the south into what appeared to be a narrow valley at the confluence of streams. Before them, a slow-moving pair of ox carts blocked the road, and Reuben reined up, stepped down and motioned to the stream. "Let's water the horses, give those carts a little time to get in the clear, and then we should make the ranch the hostler spoke about."

"Oh, yes. The Bailey ranch! Fine people, the Baileys. Will and Ann have worked hard on their place and the stages have been a help. Will said they were going to build a regular station come next spring and put folks up and feed 'em and such."

Reuben looked at the preacher. "Is it much farther?"

"Just down the bottom of the hill, no more'n a couple miles."

"Place to sleep?"

"Fine loft in the barn. Been there before, mighty fine, yessir, mighty fine!"

Reuben smiled at Elly. "Sound alright to you?"

"It does. But what about supper?" she asked.

"Oh, the Baileys will insist we have supper with

them!" explained the preacher. "And she will not accept any excuses."

They smiled at one another, glanced to the road and the oxcarts, and stepped back aboard their mounts. "Preacher, if you're of a mind, the mule there is broke to ride and if you can make yourself a seat, you're welcome to ride."

"Oh no. It's just a good stretch of the legs to the ranch and time enough to rest when the sun goes down," he explained as he stretched out to set the pace.

Reuben stood in the door of the hayloft of the big barn at Bailey's ranch, his hands on the top edge as he leaned out, looking at the sunset in the distant notch of the black timbered mountains. Elly had spread their bedrolls on the last of the hay to make a comfortable bed for the night and joined him at the window.

"What'chu thinkin'?" she asked, slipping her arm around his waist, and leaning against him.

"Oh, just thinkin' 'bout that preacher. The way he tells it, he's walked more miles than we've ridden, and he's got a lot o' walkin' ahead of him."

Elly grinned and looked up at her man. "And if I know you, you're not just saying that to be saying it. You're planning on doing something about it, aren't you?" replied Elly.

"Well, I did talk to Will about that bay geldin' in the corral yonder. He said, 'Since it's for the preacher, I'll let you have it for thirty dollars, an' I'll throw in the tack!' and it sounded like a purty good deal, so..." as he shrugged his shoulders and grinned down at Elly's uplifted face.

She pulled him close and said, "You are a good man, Reuben Grundy."

"Aw, 'tweren't much, 'sides it'll make the mule happy he won't have to carry the preacher an' watch his language!"

Elly pulled away from Reuben to look up at him with her head cocked to the side and her eyes squinting a little. "Now, how would that mule know you were gonna let the preacher ride him and how's he gonna watch his language? He only knows two words, hee and haw, so what would the preacher be objecting about?"

Reuben chuckled and reached out to grab Elly and wrestle her down to tickle her, giving the two of them a moment of laughter and fun not often enjoyed during their trek.

When they rode from the Bailey ranch, the sun was just beginning to announce the new day as it bid the darkness retreat from the grey light of early morning. They were riding into the west with the rising sun at their backs, casting long shadows before them. The stage road was above the valley floor, riding a long shoulder of the higher ridge, but they followed an ancient trail Will Bailey had told him about, a trail used by the Tabeguache Indians. The trail was narrow as it rode the steep shoulder beside the chuckling North Fork of the South Platte River. The water was clear and cold, cascading over the rocks and dancing in the ripples and rapids. The tall ponderosa competed with spruce and fir for the rationed sunlight that slowly began to share its warmth on the travelers' backs.

To their left rose the long ridge of the Platte River Mountains that rose more than three thousand feet above the valley floor, cresting with a handful of bald granite peaks that lifted grey heads into the clear blue sky, some of them well over twelve thousand feet. The black timber fell like grandma's home-stitched quilt, thick and dark and warm, sometimes hiding left over snow drifts in their shaded ravines. Yet from the trail they followed, the mountains pushed so close, it was impossible to see the crest of the ridge, towering pines and spruce hiding it well.

They rode alone, Preacher Dyer having been coerced to stay an extra day at the Bailey ranch to preach to the stage passengers and others that would be present later in the day. But they reveled in the time together, preferring their own company to any other. Reuben glanced at Elly who was smiling as she looked at him, and he asked, "What are you grinnin' about?" chuckling as he spoke.

"Oh, just how happy I am to be with you, to be here in the mountains like we dreamed, and to have such a beautiful day for our ride! Isn't it a beautiful day?"

Reuben chuckled again, shaking his head, "Yes, it is, and it's made all the more beautiful because I have a beautiful wife to share it with!"

"Oh, you devil, you!" she giggled, tucking her chin in the collar of her jacket, and looking at him with her head cocked and a broad smile painting her face. But the mood was broken when Bear jumped up, his feet on her back as he growled at something farther up the trail or in the trees.

Reuben reined up, glanced at the pup as he slipped his Sharps from the scabbard and lay it across his pommel. He searched the trees and the many rock outcroppings on either side, looking for anything that would be a danger. He heard rocks rattle that told of something moving down the hillside, probably some wild animal coming to water. He stood in his stirrups, twisting, and bending to try to see through the trees and around the stack of rocks that pushed the stream into a sharp bend. He nudged the blue forward a few steps, a glance back to Elly told her to wait. When he had a view of the stream ahead, he paused, watching, then relaxed and sat back in the saddle. He waved to Elly for her to join him and as she came alongside, he nodded to the stream. A lop eared, big nosed, moose with a long-legged gangly calf at her side, had waded into a backwater pool of the stream and was munching on some greenery she pulled from the bottom of the shallows. Elly grinned, chuckling at the efforts of the calf to nurse while his mother ate. Reuben reached to his saddle bags and brought out the binoculars, spoke softly to Elly, "I need to see where we are and what's ahead. This valley is so thick with trees, I'm feelin' a little closed in!"

Elly nodded, turning her attention back to the moose, and gave little heed to Reuben as he stepped down, slung the rifle over his shoulder and started through the trees. It was a tall granite outcropping that sat at the end of a long finger ridge that came from the higher ridge to the north. Standing about sixty feet high, the slope at the back edge offered an easier access to the crest and Reuben had already started up the loose soil, digging in his toes and leaning forward, stretching out his hands to grab rocks and brush to aid his climb. He disappeared around a shoulder of rock and Elly turned back to watch the big cow moose and her calf.

Once atop the knob of rocks, Reuben went to his belly, always concerned about skylining himself in dangerous country, and clawed his way to the crest beside a gnarly cedar. He lay his rifle to the side and lifted the binoculars. Unconcerned about any reflection, the sun at his back, he began his survey of the territory before him. The long narrow canyon carried the river on its rapid descent, cascades splashing and roaring, the sounds held close by the thick timber.

In the distance to the west, the valley widened as the shoulders and finger ridges of the higher mountains gave way and stepped back from the river. Far in the distance and north of the wider valley, he saw the bald head of a mountain he would later learn was named Mount Logan. South from that peak and across the valley, the end of the long ridge of the Platte River Mountains was marked by the Twin Cone peaks, with just the bald tips showing above the treetops.

With another look at the surroundings, he crabbed back from the crest and slipped and slid down the slope to return to Elly. She twisted around in the saddle as he returned. "The moose took off into the trees. She must have heard you rattling all the rocks and such."

Reuben grinned, slipped the binoculars back in the saddle bags, replaced the Sharps and swung back aboard Blue. "It opens up to a wider valley in another couple miles, and at the upper end, there's a trail that climbs that mountain," nodding to their left, "that Will told me about. He said it's an old Indian trail and cuts a couple miles off the journey. I reckon we'll give it a try."

"I'm following you!" she said, smiling and laughing.

THE TRAIL CRESTED A SADDLE CROSSING OF A LONG FINGER ridge that pushed into the bottom of the North Fork of the South Platte River valley. It rounded the knob of another ridge and the valley opened before them. The wide green ribbon was split by the silvery splinter of the narrow river, the tall grasses waving gently in the breeze that came from the high mountains to search the bottoms of ravines, gulches, and valleys. Reuben and Elly reined up at the edge of the ridge to sit and look at the green valley, speckled with patches of mountain flowers dancing in the wind. Blues, whites, yellows, and a few dots of red and orange, gave the touches of color that could only be credited to the Master Creator. High on the shoulders of the mountains, draws and cuts held splotches of lighter green that told of Aspen groves that would turn to gold in the fall, giving even more color to the amazing panorama.

They started to push off the ridge when Reuben said, "Dust!" and pointed farther up the valley where the stage road crested a distant finger ridge. The stage showed amidst the trailing dust cloud and Reuben grinned. "Looks like a stage is comin'!" He dropped his eyes to start on the trail, but the sudden staccato of gunfire stayed his movement. He squinted as he stood in his stirrups, then grabbed his binoculars from the saddlebags and leaned forward as he lifted the glasses. The shotgunner had turned around, laying his coach gun on the luggage up top and the blast of the big gun and the puff of grey smoke that quickly disappeared into the dust cloud told the story.

"It must be a hold-up!" said Reuben, "but I can't tell for sure, the dust!" The brown cloud rose behind the stage, making it impossible to see the pursuers. He dropped the glasses, looking around at the stage road and the environs, searching for cover. He pointed to a cluster of rocks just below the crest of the hill. "There!" and slapped heels to the roan, prompting Elly to follow close behind.

The coach was rumbling and bouncing, the six-up team showing lather around their collars and harness, tongues lolling, manes and tails flying. As they neared, Reuben dropped beside the rocks, lifting his Sharps, and taking aim. The big rifle moved with the oft-practiced hands of the sharpshooter, following the targets. Three riders were fighting the dust, firing rifles and pistols blindly at the stage trying to force it to stop. Reuben bore down on the leader, barely visible at the edge of the road, slapping legs to his mount, the brim of his hat bent under the force of the wind, a neckerchief masking his face as much to hide his identity as to protect from the dust. With his sight centered, Reuben followed the target, leading slightly, and squeezed off the shot. The big Sharps bucked and roared, spitting lead and a plume of grey smoke.

Even with the rumble of the coach, rattle of trace chains, and gunshots from the pursuers, the blast of the big gun caught the attention of the driver. "There's another'n on the hill!" he shouted to his shotgunner, nodding toward the rise with the scattered piñon and juniper. But the shotgunner turned in time to see the leader of the outlaws fall from his saddle and tumble end over end in the dust.

"NO! That fella's on our side!" he shouted, jamming two more shells into his double-barreled coach gun. He turned back, searching for the other riders, and heard the rifle shot from the hillside as the coach drew closer to the slope. The second outlaw slumped in his saddle and jerked the rein on his mount to move away from the road. The shotgunner watched as the man slid from his saddle to fall face down in the dirt beside a clump of sage. The third and last outlaw saw he was alone and jerked his mount to a stop, looking around and without any hesitation, dug spurs to his horse, lay along the neck and chased the fading cloud of dust to return from whence they came.

Reuben stood, grinned at Elly who was on one knee at the far edge of the rocks, a thin wisp of smoke coming from the barrel of her Henry. She grinned at her man and they both waved at the coach as it slowed with the Jehu leaning back on the two handfuls of reins, his foot on the big brake lever, and the coach slid to a stop. Reuben swung back aboard Blue, and he and Elly rode down the slope to see the men on the coach. The shotgunner had already dismounted the box and held the door open to the passenger compartment to let the passengers out to stretch their legs and relieve themselves.

"Hey! Hold on there, fellas, there's a lady here!" shouted Reuben, motioning to his wife, laughing at their antics. The six passengers, five men and one woman, had all exited the coach, the woman going alone to a cluster of trees nearby, but the men had not expected to see another woman and had given no thought to modesty.

But at Reuben's shout, they quickly went to the opposite side of the coach and sought cover among the sage.

Elly was giggling as they came near the driver's box and smiled up at the driver who leaned down to see the visitors.

He smiled broadly as Reuben drew near, and said, "I ain't never heard nothin' as sweet as that big boom of that thar' Sharps! You certainly saved our bacon! Buffler hunter are ye?"

"Nope, we're just passin' thru, saw your predicament, thought we'd help out."

"I thought it sounded like more'n one shooter." He frowned at Elly, saw her long blonde hair hanging below her hat, and said, "You didn't shoot, did'ju?" Elly grinned and nodded, patting the butt of her Henry that protruded from the scabbard behind her leg. He shook his head, looked at Reuben. "Don't know if I could ride with a woman that could shoot better'n me! I'd end up gettin' shot!"

"That's why I try to behave!" chuckled Reuben, eliciting a smile from Elly.

The shotgunner came from the far side of the coach, reached up to shake Reuben's hand, "We are all fired grateful for what'chu done, yessir! Them fellas were gainin' on us, and I was runnin' low on shells. If you hadn't come along, we'd prob'ly be pushin' up daisies!"

The driver leaned over and spoke a little softer, "I'm sure Mr. Hinkley, that owns this outfit, would be grateful 'nuff to wanna give you a reward. Who can we say done it?"

Reuben chuckled, glanced at Elly and back to the driver. "No need. But the name's Reuben and Elly Grundy."

"Good to meet you folks. I'm Jock Mathis, and that

there's Bristles!" The shotgunner was climbing back to the driver's box and turned to nod to the pair. "Don't concern yourself with them," nodding toward the downed outlaws, "we'll have the hostler from the station come back and tend to 'em. They'll want to catch up the horses and such."

Reuben nodded, and noticed the name painted in a circle on the door, *Hinkley and Company, Stage Line. Denver-Fairplay.* The passengers had climbed back aboard, and the woman leaned out the window and said, "Thank you!" to which Reuben responded with a nod. The driver lay out his bullwhip, cracking it as loud as a pistol shot, to start the team on the way and Bristles waved to the pair as the stage pulled away.

Reuben looked at his woman. "Whatsay we find us a place to have a noonin'? I'm cravin' some coffee."

"What'chu fixing for our meal?" asked Elly, grinning at her man.

"Leftovers, what else?" answered Reuben as he nudged the roan toward the trail that pointed up the narrow tree-lined draw. They stopped at the first confluence of run-off creek beds where enough of a clearing offered deep grass for the animals, a trickle of water from a spring in an aspen grove and some tall ponderosa for shade. Using a handful of the long dry needles from the ponderosa, and some dead fall branches, they had a small, hat-sized smokeless fire going and the coffee pot with spring water growing warm. Reuben produced a pouch with a handful of biscuits and sausage from Ann Bailey and their early breakfast. With the frying pan hot, the sausage shed enough grease to soften the biscuits and their fresh coffee topped off their hastily fashioned noon feast.

"We're gonna need some fresh meat soon," suggested Elly, finishing up her biscuits.

"Maybe we can get us a deer toward evenin' when they come to water," replied Reuben, rising to stretch and check on the animals. He walked toward the horses, glanced to the sun to calculate the remaining hours of daylight, then looked up the long draw to the bald ridge high above. A sudden rifle shot startled him and he dropped to the ground as he spun around to look behind him and saw a laughing Elly holding her Henry one handed at her side and pointing at him.

"Boy, did you jump! You'd think I shot at you instead o' them turkeys," she explained, nodding to the edge of the trees near the bottom of the draw. She turned and started down the slight slope to retrieve her bounty and held up a fat but headless turkey, wings draping, and tail feathers fanned. She grinned and started back up the hill, smiling and laughing. "I thought a turkey would be a nice change of fare!" She held the turkey high. "What'dya think?"

"He's a fat one alright! You coulda warned me!"

"If I'da made a sound they would have scattered!" She dropped her prize to the ground, leaned her rifle against a big rock and poured herself another cup of coffee. She looked at the bird, shook her head. "I'll get him dressed and plucked while you get the animals ready and packs loaded, and we can head on out. We'll need to stop a little early, so we'll have time to roast him proper!" she explained.

The trail followed the dry creek bed, a sandy bottomed trail made by eons of snowmelt and traffic of timberline deer and high-country elk herds. It wound through the thick aspen groves that claimed the moist soil of the wide gully that lay between the long finger ridges coming from the long line of close hugging mountains. The crest of the ridge was bald, rising above timberline and as they broke from the trees, they had their first glimpse of the high-altitude windy pines, known as Bristlecone pines. Elly stared at the trees whose branches were all on one side as if waving to a distant friend. The opposite side of the tree trunk was wind blasted red from standing against the icy winds of the high country.

"Hey, look at that!" declared Reuben as he stepped down from his saddle.

Elly pushed the Appy near Blue, slid down from her saddle, caught Bear as he jumped to her arms, almost knocking her down, and set him down. She stepped beside Reuben to look at the vista before them. As the tall ridge tumbled below to a rumpled carpet of rolling timber-covered hills, to their right and framing the park, marched a long line of granite peaked mountains, each holding patches of snow above timberline as they stood guard over the wide and fertile South Park. The hip hanging garments of black timber seemed to be one long blanket of pines, separating the towering peaks from the rolling foothills that bordered the park. The wide park showed a random pattern of green and tan with brief interruptions of juniper covered ridges and roundtops. To the west, more mountains, even higher, stood like a second and third line of defense, formidable obstacles to anyone or anything that dared to penetrate the interior of the Rockies.

They stood speechless for several long moments, taking in the amazing views, knowing this was just a random sampling of God's amazing creation. Reuben shook his head and said, "God must have had fun makin' all this!"

Elly smiled, nodding. "Ummhummm. I never imagined such beauty. When I heard about the Rocky Mountains, I could not envision how anything could be bigger than the hills of the Ozarks and their like, but this!"

They sat on the ground, side by side and holding one another's hand, looking over the grand view until Reuben suggested, "At the bottom of the hills yonder," pointing to the west along the edge of the mountains, "where the stage road comes out, the preacher said there was a station called Kenosha. He said they have good rooms, food, and company. He also said he was plannin' on bein' there come Sunday to preach to folks."

"Oh, he did? Well, tomorrow's Sunday, so he better get a move on; us too," answered Elly, rising with the rein of her Appy in her hand. "I'd like to hear him preach. Been quite a while since we been in church anywhere!"

"Not that long. We were in church in Julesburg!"

"That was a dance! Not a preaching service!"

"Oh, yeah. But didn't we go to church there also?" asked Reuben, uncertain of his memory. Elly just smiled, nodded, and mounted up.

E lly led the way toward the mouth of the cut that pointed to the valley below. The dim trail showed amidst the thick cushion plants that appeared as a soft green carpet sporting tiny pink blossoms. Elly was enamored with the tiny plants, reining up beside a patch of Skunkweed that was sometimes called the Sky Pilot showing blue-violet cone shaped flowers stretching toward the warm sun. Across the way was another purple blossomed plant that appeared to have fringe on each of its blossoms. Random pinpoints of pink heralded the low growing bitterroot, and a little farther, tiny clusters of blue forget-me-nots standing all of three inches tall. She sat still, waiting for Reuben, and leaned on her pommel for a good look around at the different terrain of the high-country tundra, unique to the alpine reaches of the Rocky Mountains. She smiled as Reuben came alongside and pointed out the pale blue clusters, "I don't know what they're called here, but they look a lot like the forget-me-nots back home, just smaller."

"That green moss and the lichen on the rocks are certainly different than anythin' we've seen before," added Reuben, enjoying the brief stop to take in the wonders of the land.

"I heard water and I think there's a stream in the bottom of that draw that leads into the aspen. You take the lead in case there's a bear in there," she stated, eyebrows lifted as she moved side to side as if to see through the distant grove of aspen.

Reuben grinned and spoke to Blue, "Well boy, sounds like we been elected to bear duty. So, let's get a move on so if we see one, we can outrun him, and he'll chase the slower, more tender female and her pup!"

"You just wait! Me'n Bear will get you when you least expect it!" she called after him, laughing, as he moved away, starting down the dim trail that led into the trees.

The white barked aspen with their light green, always fluttering in the breeze, leaves were most often called Quakies because of that constant movement of the leaves. The trees, white bark showing black scars where branches had broken or animals had clawed or rubbed velvet off horns, grew close together, saplings stretching for sunlight alongside bigger mature trees with trunks as much as twenty inches in diameter. The light green canopy seemed to wave visitors through the maze of towering trunks and leaf-strewn carpet. Reuben thought he saw movement and brought Blue to a stop, the mule mimicking his friend as both stood quiet. Reuben caught glimpses of tan and brown passing through the trees, but the trees were too thick to glimpse more than a few inches of color. Yet the swaying of the trees, moving in concert with the unidentified animal told Reuben that whatever it was, it was big enough to push through the close-growing trees, moving them aside as it walked.

Reuben nudged Blue forward, slipping his Sharps from the scabbard, and earing back the hammer as he lay the weapon across the pommel. Without taking his eyes from the last point of view, he slowly advanced. A break in the trees gave him a quick view of two animals as they were pushed farther by a larger third beast with the same tan color and dark brown chest and legs. *"Elk!"* whispered Reuben. When the third bull stepped into the slight clearing, Reuben caught his breath as he saw the monstrous animal, head high, massive antlers with strips of velvet hanging as tattered shreds moving about as the bull shook his head side to side. He had been using the passage through the trees to help shed the velvet from the massive rack, and now sought to shake the dangling matter free. He dropped his head, driving the long tines into the soil, bellowing, and grunting from the effort, churning the soil as he sought to tear the last of the velvet from his antlers. The big bull stopped, lifted his head looking around as if he had heard something that alarmed him, then trotted off into the trees, disappearing in the thick grove.

As Elly came through the thicket, Reuben nodded toward the churned-up dirt and said, "You missed quite a sight! There was a big bull elk followin' a couple others, tryin' to get the velvet off his antlers and plowed up this clearin' like a farmer with a plow! He was a big un'!"

"I was watching a bobcat chasing a big-footed, long-eared rabbit! What do they call those, snowshoes?"

"If he had big feet and ears like you said, then yeah, he was a snowshoe. Did the bobcat catch him?"

"Dunno, the last I saw, the rabbit was winning, and the bobcat was mad about it!"

They both chuckled at the antics of the animals, and Reuben added, "Maybe after we get out of these aspen, we might spot a deer in the willows and get some fresh meat."

"Then I'll let you do the shooting and I'll do the cooking," she resolved, giving Reuben a nod to take to the trail. He slipped the Sharps into the scabbard and started off.

Both the now chuckling creek and the trail bent back to the north, blockaded by a long ridge with scattered juniper and buck brush covering its slopes. They were beside the thick willows when Reuben held up a hand to stop, motioning farther downstream and twisting around in his seat to whisper, "There's a couple deer yonder, might be our chance to get some fresh meat. You wanna give it a try?"

Elly shook her head. "Nope. Like I said, you shoot 'em, I'll cook 'em."

Reuben chuckled, slipped the Henry from the scabbard under his left leg, choosing the smaller and lighter weapon over the Sharps. Elly slid to the ground, accepted the rein from Reuben and found a seat on the creek bank to watch the horses and mule graze the deep grass while Reuben started his stalk.

She leaned back to take the sun on her face when a splash in the water brought her up. She smiled when she saw the ripple from a widening circle caused by a trout taking a bug and watched as several more brook trout lazily rode the current behind a big rock, waiting for more tasty tidbits. She couldn't help but think how simple life seemed to be for God's creatures, and how hectic it can be for people. She had been trying to clear her mind of the image of the man she shot as he tumbled from his saddle to lie unmoving in the dust and sage beside the stage road. She had killed before, but usually by reflex, while this was deliberate and purposeful although needful. It was as if her heart ached, the dull pain in her chest, at the thought of killing someone. She shook her head as she wondered if the man had a family, or a sweetheart. Certainly he had dreams, maybe plans and hope for the future. *What if he had a family? Children, maybe.* She was startled by the sound of a rifle shot coming from the lower reaches of the creek, probably Reuben taking a deer. She cleared her mind as she stood, went to her Appy and made a hop to reach the stirrup and swung aboard. Bending down to catch the rein of Blue, she looked at the mule. "C'mon mule. You've got some packing to do!" and started down the little creek, searching for Reuben.

They made quick work of field dressing the deer until Reuben suggested, "Why don't we just take the meat, no reason to have the rest. We'll use the hide to wrap the cuts, and when we get to the station, we might share it with those folks and the preacher."

Elly smiled. "Sounds fine to me!"

Within a short while, the bundle of meat was atop the packsaddle, and they were on the way. To their left, a bald saddle crossing beckoned, and they turned back to the west to cross the ridge, the far side thick with aspen and a meandering trail through the grove. Once free of the quakies they were at the side of the stage road that bent to the south, siding another small creek, to round the big knob that faced the vast South Park. The bald face of the knob offered an unhindered view of the wide park and they stopped again, stepped down, and took in the view. Reuben pointed to the south where the thin line of the stage road cut the park. "Looks like the road goes all the way through the park, looks to be a fork yonder where a side road cuts back to the west. From what Will and the preacher said, Kenosha station should be somewhere along the face of this here mountain," pointing along the edge of the trees that rode the crest of the foothills.

He leaned forward, and took a couple steps down the slope, shaded his eyes and pointed. "There it is, I can see it yonder!" He walked back to Elly. "Let's get a move on and we'll be there in, oh, maybe an hour or sooner."

"Suits me! Preacher Dyer said they had some rooms for travelers and if we get there before a stage stops, maybe we can get one!" She picked up Bear, set him atop the bedroll and haversack, and led her appy beside a big rock that offered her an easy way to mount. Once aboard, Bear pushed his nose between her elbow and her side, and she quickly gave him a hug and let him snuggle close. Reuben nudged Blue back to the side of the road, and they crossed to the high side, to follow the road to the stage station.

9 / ESPINOSAS

"**T**his, this is where we begin *la Revolución!*" declared Felipe Espinosa, scowling at his younger brother, Vivián José Espinosa. "That man is a judge, and his death will spread fear among all the gringos!" The two men sat their horses atop a flat timber-covered mesa and were overlooking the narrow valley that carried Hardscrabble creek toward the Arkansas River, several miles north. On the shoulder of the far bank and rise to the wide plateau, a sawmill with a noisy steam engine powering the big circular saw, was shutting down operation for the day. Two men had already mounted their horses and left for the day, but the owner, Judge William Bruce, was finishing the shut-down of the engine, releasing the remaining pressure and closing up the building.

Felipe, the older of the brothers, grinned broadly, showing his toothy grin and lantern jaw. Standing about three inches shy of six feet, his whiskery face and curly hair were shaded by his broad-brimmed sombrero. His leather jacket covered a linsey Woolsey button shirt tucked into canvas britches that were also tucked into knee high boots. He wore a Remington Navy revolver in a holster that also held a silver capped knife. Across his pommel lay a Henry .44 rifle. Vivián was dressed much the same but wore *chaparreras* over his britches and his face bore only a mustache. Both men had piercing black eyes that were accented by their dark countenance and shaded faces under the big sombreros.

Felipe led them off the mesa, crossed the creek and came up to the sawmill from the far side, masking their approach from the judge. They slipped silently to the ground, dropping their reins to ground tie the horses, and at Felipe's motion, Vivián went to the right and Felipe to the left, circling the building to come at the judge from both sides. Felipe approached first and the judge, surprised, looked up. "Sorry, I'm just shuttin' it down. But if you need some lumber, I might be able to provide enough from my stock."

"No, no. I do not need any lumber. I have come to fulfill the vision given me by the blessed Virgin Mary," explained Felipe, flashing his toothy grin.

The judge frowned. "I don't know what you mean."

"You gringos have taken everything! First you steal our land, tell us our ancient land grants are no good. Then you send your soldiers to attack our homes, rape my wife and sister, kill my children, and burn our home! But it will be no more!" He raised his voice almost to a shout, "The blessed virgin has told me to kill one hundred gringos for every member of my family that they killed!" As he spoke, he drew the pistol from his holster and held it at his side and now lifted it as he snarled at the man before him.

The judge stood, eyes wide and holding his hands out before him as if to stop any bullet with his hands. "But,

but, I had nothin' to do with that! Where did that happen?" he pleaded, hoping to dissuade his attackers.

"In San Judas de Tadeo, what you call the San Luis valley. Land that has been in our family for generations, given to us in a land grant. By the Treaty of Guadalupe, it was to always be our land until you greedy gringos wanted it for yourselves. They ruined our family, took everything from us, even the food from our mouths, then they destroyed my family and my home! You will be the first to pay, gringo!" He growled the words, stepped forward slightly to look directly into the frightened eyes of the judge and pulled the trigger. The bullet struck Bruce in the chest, knocking him to the ground, but he wasn't dead. Vivián grabbed an axe that leaned against the building, straddled the man and as the judge again struggled to lift his hands, Vivián Espinosa screamed, *"Viva la Revolución!"* as the axe fell and split the judge's skull.

Vivián stepped off the body as Felipe dropped to his knees, eyes flaring, teeth showing, as he drove his knife deep into the chest of the dead man, cutting and splitting, until he reached into the cavity and cut the man's heart free. He held the bloody trophy high, shouting, *"Viva la Revolución!"* He tossed the bloody heart aside and began carving the crucifix on the bare chest of the dead man. Satisfied, he stood, spat on the body, and turned to his brother. "We go to find more!"

Vivián looked to the south across the wide expanse of the Arkansas valley, pointed to the distant Pike's Peak. "There!" I have heard of the gold rush! We will kill gringos and grow rich!"

"Si! Es Bueno!" responded Felipe, starting to the creek to wash off the blood.

"*MI HERMANO*," BEGAN VIVIÁN AS THEY RODE TOGETHER across the sagebrush and buffalo grass covered flat, pointing toward the towering Pikes Peak, "you have said this is the start of *la Revolución*, but what about the gringos we killed in the valley? You know, the ones that had taken the land from our people? Do they not count as some of the number in your vision, the one hundred for every one of our family?"

Felipe grinned, looking at his brother, "*Si, si*. They count, but how many were there?"

"*Veinte*, maybe more."

"And we have so many more, do we not?" asked Felipe.

"*Si, si*, many more," chuckled Vivián, reassured.

They made camp on the banks of the Arkansas river, well protected by the thick cottonwoods and sharp bluff on the east bank and the rolling adobe hills on the west. As they sat by the small fire in the rock ring, Vivián used the light of the embers and stars to write in his journal about the events and thoughts of the day. It had become his habit since his wife had been killed by the soldiers and he had vengefully killed one of the men that had raped her before he fled with his brother. It was his way of talking to her, sharing all his thoughts and the way he and his brother were seeking the vengeance they believed was their right. As he wrote, he glanced up to see his brother was also writing, and he asked, "What is it you write, *mi hermano*?"

Felipe chuckled. "I am writing a letter to the governor, Evans."

"The governor?" asked Vivián, disbelieving.

"*Si, si*. I am telling him what we are doing, and what we will do. That we will kill six hundred Anglos to pay for what they did to our family. And that we will also kill him unless he gives us, and all our family that will join us, pardons and five thousand acres of land in the San Luis Valley. If he does not, we will continue to kill Anglos!" He laughed as he held up the paper, waving it in the firelight.

It was just after midday when they spotted a thin wisp of smoke rising from the small stovepipe atop the big barn-like structure, but the sound of a steam engine of sorts came from within and the stacks of lumber to the side told the brothers this was a sawmill, not unlike the one where they killed the judge. It too sat near a creek, this one known as Fountain Creek, for the mill had been powered by the water before they purchased the steam engine. They watched from the trees, saw two men load lumber into a buckboard, climb aboard and with a wave to another, drove off.

Felipe looked at Vivián, "I think there is just one other. We will watch for a while, and if there is only one, we will take him."

It was just a short while later that the sounds of shutting down the steam powered sawmill were heard and the brothers knew the man was alone, so they pushed from the trees to approach the mill. The mill operator came from the building, saw the two approaching and lifted his hand to wave, smiling. "Howdy men! You needin' some lumber are ya?" He stood before the building watching the men as they neared, "I'm Henry Harkens, and this here's my sawmill. If we don't have what'chu need, we can cut it for you."

The brothers reined up and stepped down, Felipe grinning broadly. "No señor, we do not need any lumber, nor do we need you to cut any. We will do our own cutting!"

Harkens frowned. "I don't understand. I don't let

folks use my sawmill, that's just for me and my men. It's a very expensive piece of machinery and it's hard to learn."

"*Si*, but you can give us some directions."

"Certainly, where you headin'?"

"We heard there was a road that would take us to the area called South Park, where the goldfields are, do you know of such a road?"

"Easy. See those foothills yonder," pointing to the west and the long line of timbered foothills that lay below Pikes Peak. "Just follow the edge until you're a little past the Peak, and you'll find the road that cuts through those hills and goes o'er Wilkerson Pass. 'Bout a day's ride to the road, another couple days to the park. Now, as far as doin' your own cuttin', I don't let folks do their own cuttin', not on my equipment."

"No, *señor*, you don't understand," cackled Felipe as he withdrew his knife from the scabbard at his waist, touching the razor-sharp blade with his finger, drawing blood. "My knife, it is very sharp, you see. And with it, I will cut out your heart!" As he spoke the word heart, he lunged forward, driving the blade into the man's chest, just below his rib cage, twisting it and moving the blade back and forth, snarling in the sawyer's face, watching his life fade from his startled wide eyes. "I weel keel you gringos!" He stepped back, letting the man fall to the ground, blood pulsing from the wound.

While Felipe was busy killing the man, Vivián searched for an axe, found one and returned to repeat his action of before. The blade split the sawyer's head and two additional swings decapitated it from the body. Felipe looked at his brother, shook his head, and began cutting the bloody shirt away to reveal the hairy chest. He greedily cut away the flesh, reached for the heart and

B.N. RUNDELL

cut it free. He sat back to look at the chest upon which
he carved two crucifixes. He stood, looking at his work
and spat on the body, grabbed the tattered remains of
the man's shirt and wiped the blade of his knife and
cleaned his bloody hands. With a glance to his brother,
he mounted up and motioned to the creek, and they
splashed across the shallow stream and looked to the
foothills that lay below Pikes Peak and started along the
east edge of the timbered foothills, searching for the
road they knew would take them to South Park and the
valley of the goldfields.

10 / BLOODLUST

The Pikes Peak Gold rush had created the demand for more and better wagon roads which in turn gave birth to many wagon road construction companies. The Denver, Auraria and South Park Wagon Road Company, and the Denver and San Luis Valley Wagon Road company competed for the contract from Colorado City to Fairplay, over Ute Pass. The road was already in use by the stage lines and freight lines carrying passengers and supplies from Colorado City when Felipe and Vivián José Espinosa rode through the timber covered hills on their way to South Park.

The brothers traveled the well-used road but avoided the freighters and stages or any other travelers that were in groups. It was coming on dusk, the road riding a slight shoulder of the timber covered rolling foothills with a narrow green valley carrying the shallow Fountain creek, and Felipe saw the smoke of a campfire rising from the edge of the pines. Tall ponderosa stood above the fir and spruce, a grassy slope falling away from the trees, and movement caught the older brother's eye as two tethered horses grazed on the tall green grass. He

61

grinned as he nodded to his brother. "*Mi hermano*, perhaps there will be a camp we can share."

Vivián grinned, his eyes becoming slits as he snarled, "*Si, si.* And the blade of my axe is thirsty for blood."

As they neared the camp, Felipe called out, "Hello the camp!" the customary greeting when approaching the camp of strangers, used to prevent gunfire and give the campers warning of someone approaching, supposedly friendly.

A prospector looking man with heavy brogans, high water britches held up with braces over a dark plaid shirt, open to expose the faded red union suit, stepped from the trees. His meaty paws held a Colt revolving shotgun. A heavy black beard with shots of grey showing, bobbed as the man answered, "Come in if you're friendly. Keep your hands away from any weapons or I'll empty yore saddle!"

Felipe glanced to Vivián, back to the man and held his free hand high, lifting the reins above the pommel as he said, "No, *señor*, we only look to share your fire. We have some coffee and tortillas to share."

"Tortillas? You fellas Mex, are ya?"

"*Si, señor*, we are up from Mexico on our way to see if we can find some of the gold everyone else is after," he explained as they rode into the campsite. Felipe started to step down, then paused, looked at the man, "Can we get down?"

"Sure, sure," replied the man, nodding to his partner who was kneeling at the fire and tending to something that was in the pot. He moved to the log by the fire, setting the shotgun down to lean it against the log before he seated himself beside it.

Felipe swung his leg over the rump of his horse, nodding to his brother who was between Felipe and the woods. Vivián also swung down, putting himself between the horses as Felipe turned toward the men, his pistol in hand as he grinned malevolently at the two surprised men. Without another word, he cocked the hammer, the clicking sound freezing the men, then dropped the hammer, the pistol bucking and barking as he fired into the chest of the first man. The shots from the pistol were echoed by those from the pistol in Vivián's hand as he shot the kneeling man. The man at the fire, eyes wide with fear, fell into the fire, splattering the pot into the flames. The commotion startled the horses of the brothers, making them jerk back, heads lifted, as they back stepped, but the angry brothers pulled the reins taut, as they looked at their victims. The first man had tumbled over backwards to fall in a heap behind the log.

"Pull him out of the fire, he stinks!!" declared Felipe, glaring at his brother.

Vivián grabbed the man by the ankles, pulled him from the flames, and grabbed his axe, grinning and mumbling as he moved. He straddled the smoking carcass, lifted the axe over his head and brought it down to split the man's skull, the detritus spilling into the coals of the fire. He glanced to his brother who dragged the body of the first prospector away from the log and sat astraddle of the form, stripping off the shirt and union suit to begin his carving.

They stripped the bodies of anything of value, took the men's weapons, and set the horses free. They knew it would be too easy to identify the horses and chose not to be hindered with the extra animals. As dusk settled over the foothills, they rode from the camp staying on the main road that bent to the west and cut through a smattering of aspen and pine as it climbed from the lower foothills to eventually mount to the crest of Ute Pass. A wide flat with scattered buffalo and Indian grasses, now dry brown, that waved in the shading light of dusk, marked the crest of the old Indian trail that had been followed for eons. The low rolling hills of the high-country flat land offered little in the way of cover and the brothers kept riding until a finger ridge came from the timbered foothills on the north, shadowing a dry sandy gulch that beckoned.

AS THE SUN CRESTED THE HILLS TO THE EAST, THE brothers were on the road, putting distance between them and the scenes of their atrocities. They kept a steady pace, never stopping except for brief graze and water for the horses. As the sun was lowering in the west, they crested Wilkerson Pass and the South Park opened expansively before them, the distant mountains of the Mosquito Range framed the west edge of the park. They crested a small knob that overlooked a dense thicket of aspen on the west edge of the bluff and a shout from below caught their attention. As they watched, a lone rider pushed several head of cattle from the trees, hollering as he drove the stubborn animals, and was starting them down a wide gulch that opened to the flats below. The man stepped down from his horse and led the animal to the edge of the trees, disappearing from the view of the brothers.

Felipe looked at his brother, grinning his jack-o-lantern grin with his big teeth, and Vivián knew what he intended. The brothers pushed off the knob, separating to move on either side of the thicket, and soon came upon the lone rider. He had stopped to relieve himself and was biting off a piece of jerky as he looked up at Felipe, the first to come into view.

"Howdy, friend! Didn't 'spect to see nobody up hyar." He stretched out his free hand, "I'm J.D. Addleman, this is my ranch hyar," nodding to the wide flats below. He pointed to a site at the edge of the trees coming from the east. "My place is over yonder, by them trees there. Ain't much yet, but we're buildin' it up a little at a time."

Felipe had leaned forward on his pommel, his arms crossed, and shoulders hunched. He nodded as the man spoke, then said, "*Si Bueno*, I am Felipe, and that," pointing to his brother coming around the point of trees, "is *mi hermano*, Vivián. We are here for your heart."

The rancher frowned, "I'm afraid I don't understand. Your accent made it sound like you were here for my heart. That can't be right."

"Oh, but it is," laughed Felipe, bringing his pistol around and pulling the trigger to shoot the rancher. The bullet struck his solar plexus, causing the man to stagger back, looking down at the blossoming red on his shirt with wide startled eyes, and with a fading look to his murderer, he crumpled to the ground. The brothers repeated their actions of before, using the rancher's bedroll and canteen to clean themselves and their weapons, and riding away from the thicket of aspen, facing the setting sun as they looked for either a campsite or more victims.

UNFAMILIAR WITH SOUTH PARK AND ANXIOUS TO AVOID any place that had several people, the brothers chose to travel north, always wanting to put distance and time between them and their victims. It had become their way to choose their targets by number and location, never going against more than two, and always in a secluded site. Although willing to leave no doubt as to their way of killing and to make others fearful, they were careful that no one would be alive to tell of their identity. Their desire for anonymity required them to hide themselves whenever nearing anything resembling civilization.

In South Park during the gold rush, all the strikes had been on the west edge of the park and in the mountains that lay as foothills of the Mosquito Range, but the sight of snow in the high country, easily seen from anywhere in the park, was forbidding to men who had spent their lives in hot and sunny dryland with the closest mountains the distant Sangre de Cristo range. South Park was framed by the Mosquito Range on the west, the Platte River mountains on the north, the foothills of the Arkansas River on the south and what some were calling the Tarryall mountains with the Puma Hills below on the east. The brothers kept the lower foothills of the Puma hills on their right, bound for the Tarryall Creek that would take them to the upper end of the Park and then they would move south in search of victims of their Revolution.

11 / STATION

The imposing two-story log building stood on the flat shoulder before the large barn, two outbuildings and the pole corral that held about a dozen horses. The chosen site for the Kenosha house overlooked the wide expanse of South Park with the backdrop of the Front Range mountains that held the distant Mt. Evans and more. It sat like the head of the cradle that rocked between the Mosquito Range to the west and the rolling foothills to the east, with a glimmer of the Sangre de Cristo range at its foot. Grasslands and rumpled ridges and round tops provided the blanket of cover that was seamed by the rustic carved roads to prospect holes and hastily-built towns.

When Reuben and Elly rode into the yard before the Kenosha House, they saw several hostlers busy at the barn and corrals, one coach sat in the shade of the barn getting swept out and wiped down in anticipation of the next day's ride. The door of the station was propped open, taking in the cool evening breeze, and the interior showed bright with the windows thrown open and sunlight pouring into the otherwise dark interior. They reined up at the hitchrail near the door and stepped down, Elly dropping the pup, that now was knee high, to the ground and stepped to the stoop where Reuben waited for her to enter first.

As soon as they darkened the doorway, a cheerful and friendly voice, though somewhat gravelly, bid them welcome with, "Howdy folks! Welcome to the Kenosha House. Dinner's on at the table yonder, find a seat and fill your plate!" The greeter was a husky-built man, whiskers on his jowls, a twinkle in his eyes that sparkled from under a single bushy brow, and sparse hair that went every which way. He was not the typical image of a hotelier nor a cook, but more like the prospector, stage driver, or hostler that he used to be before building the station.

Reuben chuckled at the man's greeting, "We'll do that, but first, do you have any rooms available?"

"For a price! They're in short supply and great demand, so . . . it'll take two dollars to get one!"

"That'll do," answered Reuben, digging out a ten-dollar gold piece from the Clark, Gruber and Company bank and mint in Denver City. He handed it to the greeter, introducing himself, "I'm Reuben Grundy and this is my wife, Elly."

The man nodded. "And I'm George Harriman," looking at the coin and back to Reuben. "I'll get your change in a bit," holding up flour covered hands, "go ahead and get yourself a seat," nodding toward the long table that already had ten people seated and eating. They joined the crowd and were on the receiving end of several less than congenial stares, but most paid little attention to the couple as they sat side by side at the end of the table. Within a short while the group dispersed one by one, going outside to the porch to take in the cool evening colors, or retiring to their room or to the loft in the barn. An odd assortment of benches, chairs and stools provided seating for those that wanted them, while Reuben and Elly sat close on the edge of the porch, Bear at Elly's side, their feet dangling over the edge.

A rather portly and talkative man had been regaling the group with tales of his travels as a drummer to the settlements in the goldfields and had started into a story that was a little more colorful than most and Reuben interrupted his telling, "Excuse me, sir, but by your own admission in the telling of your exploits, you apparently have forgotten the proper decorum when in mixed company. I'm sure it was a slip of the tongue and an oversight, but I would ask you to show a little more courtesy when there is a lady present."

The man stuttered and stumbled, clearing his voice, and coming to his feet. He was dressed as a drummer, or what folks in the city would say, he was attired as a gentleman, with linen checkered trousers held up over a white cotton three button shirt with brown leather braces. He also wore a brocade vest and had lain his frock coat on the back of the chair he vacated. He stepped toward Reuben, nodded toward Elly. "If you mean that person that is dressed like a man, armed like a man, and keeps company with animals, then I see no reason for decorum!"

Reuben glanced at Elly as she put her hand on his arm to calm him a little, but Reuben rose to his feet, standing before the vulgar would-be ruffian, clenching his fists, and trying to hold his temper. He was surprised at the manner of the man for this was the west, and women, no matter their background or place, were held in high regard and respected. It was unusual for anyone to act in a degrading manner to any woman, especially when she was obviously accompanied and probably married to the man beside her.

Reuben often struggled with his temper for he knew that when it flared, there would be trouble and most often someone would either take a severe beating, or someone would die. Reuben looked at the drummer, a van dyke style mustache and beard adorning an otherwise close shaven face, dark curly hair hanging over his ears and collar, his feet shuffling as he flexed his arms, readying for a fight. He looked at Reuben. "You are armed, I am not."

Reuben grinned, slipped the Remington from the holster with one hand, the tomahawk with the other, dropping them to Elly. He had left his leather jacket across the saddle earlier, and now stood before the man, buckskin britches over his moccasins, loose linen shirt giving little hinderance to his arms as he stepped to the side, watching the blowhard.

"Hear, hear!" shouted Harriman from the doorway. "If you're gonna mix it up, get off the porch! There's room enough in the yard for your frolickin'!"

Reuben motioned with his hand, offering the drummer to take to the steps first, then followed him down the few steps into the wide grassy yard. As he came down the steps, he gave the yard a quick survey for any obstacles, or possible weapons or aids in the coming fracas. The drummer turned to face him, grinning, and moving his feet back and forth, holding his upturned fists on extended arms before him. Reuben had seen fighters that thought they were skilled in the art of fisticuffs take that stance, but he had learned the stance was a waste of effort. While with the Sharpshooters, the group of men passed their free time in boxing matches with one another. Reuben had learned from a very experienced boxer that hailed from New York where he had been a part of the Bowery Boys and was the right-hand man to William 'Bill the Butcher' Poole, the founder of the gang. His friend was also a member of the police and boxed professionally in his free time. It was from him, Bucky Yamin, that Reuben learned the skills of a boxer and a bouncer.

The drummer started moving sideways, to circle around Reuben but Reuben just watched, his hands at his side as he watched the drummer's movements and eyes. He had learned to watch for 'tells' for most fighters give themselves away before they make a move, either with their eyes, their stance, or their body language. The drummer dropped his left shoulder slightly as he cocked his right arm, and Reuben watched as the fist came his way. Reuben moved his head just enough for the blow to miss and stepped away as the drummer tried to bring a left as an uppercut and follow-through, both missing and causing the man to stumble forward, his head on a swivel looking for his quarry.

Reuben was behind him, chuckling and watching as the man spun around, lowered his fists and started charging toward Reuben, arms spread, thinking to bear him to the ground, but again Reuben twisted to the side, slapping the man's outstretched arm aside and bringing his knee up to the man's hip and stomach, spinning him around and causing him to stumble backwards frantically trying to catch his footing before he fell. When he was again upright and in his stance, he growled to Reuben, "Why don'tchu stand still, you afraid?"

Reuben chuckled, circling the man, planning his

moves, backing him toward the porch. The man back peddled, eyes flaring watching Reuben as he bobbed back and forth, occasionally feinting with a right jab. When the man was near the porch, Reuben feinted with a left, caught the man dodging the feint and connected with a roundhouse right that caught the man just under his ear, causing him to stumble to the side and fall. Before he could get up, Reuben was astraddle of him, his slightly more than six-foot frame, long arms and legs making his movements almost natural. He grabbed the drummer's braces pulling the man's britches up tight, making the man squirm and swing his arms wildly. But Reuben had the edge of the britches, the collar of his shirt and jerked him back as Reuben found a seat on an upturned length of unsplit firewood and brought the man across his lap. In one quick move, Reuben snapped the braces, breaking them from the man's trousers and jerked his trousers down to his knees, exposing his drawers, and grabbed a flat piece of firewood kindling and gave the man a proper spanking. With every blow, the man yelled and cussed, and Reuben said, "Watch your language or I won't stop! Every curse word gets another swat!"

The drummer kicked his feet like a spoiled child, swung his arms, but Reuben had one leg over the man's legs just above his knees, and his left arm and elbow at the back of the man's neck, as he swung the paddle with all his force. The smack of the paddle elicited howls of laughter from everyone on the porch, giggles from Elly, and moans and barks from Bear. When the screaming and shouting from the drummer subsided to nothing more than muffled moans with every blow, Reuben said, "Maybe next time, you'll mind your manners, especially around womenfolk," and tossed the paddle aside as he rolled the man to the ground, standing tall over the scrambling and totally embarrassed figure who fought to pull his britches up and fasten his braces. Tears were streaming down his reddened face as he gritted his teeth and glared at Reuben, but he knew any move he made would be easily countered by his opponent who had easily proven himself able to handle anyone.

The drummer, head hanging, wiped his face and stomped up the stairs, went to his jacket and fumbled with the frock coat's pockets. Reuben was coming up the stairs, but Elly had carefully watched the man, knowing he was embarrassed but also bent on revenge and might try something. As he reached for the jacket pockets, Elly caught a glimpse of the butt of a small pistol and quickly brought her Colt to bear on the man, "You do it, you die!" she stated, without raising her voice, but giving a command as to a recalcitrant child.

The drummer's eyes flared, then squinted as he released the pistol to fall into the coat pocket. With a glare to Reuben and a glance to Elly, he stomped off the porch and walked to the barn where his bedroll waited in the loft beside others of the stage.

"You watch that man, you've made yourself an enemy and he can't show his face anywhere now that this story won't be told. He's a bad un, I've seen him before and he'll try to get even, you can put money on it," declared the station owner, Harriman.

"Well, maybe he'll stay for the preachin' in the mornin' and the Lord will straighten him out, or maybe the preacher will," offered Reuben, grinning.

"I think the good Lord gave up on that'n a long time ago, and as for the preacher man, he's been known to

confront just about anyone on their way of life, but
that'n doesn't have a conscience, I'll warrant," added
Harriman, turning back to the station door, throwing a
towel over his shoulder, and going to the basin to do the
dishes. He mumbled, "I'm gonna hafta get me some help.
I hate doin' dishes!"

The stagecoach slid to a stop behind the lathered team, the billowing dust cloud enveloping the coach and horses making the driver and shotgunner fan the air before the faces as they spit and coughed. With the cloud of dust trailing them all the way from Red Hill, they had neckerchiefs over their mouth and nose, but had dropped them in favor of fresh cool morning air, yet the brown cloud covered them although for just a moment. The doors did not open, nor the curtains rise. The passengers had learned to wait until the coach quit rocking and the dust had cleared before crowding out to find the accommodations for the stop.

As the shotgunner climbed down, the driver tossed the reins to the hostler and followed his messenger to the ground. They opened the doors for the passengers and the shotgunner offered his hand, a tipped hat, and a smile to an attractive woman as she exited the coach. Her red hair was stacked high, crowned with a flowered bonnet and her checkered gingham dress was adorned with brocade stitching and embroidered flowers that matched those on her bonnet. She smiled widely as she accepted the man's hand, stepping down to dust herself off and sashay into the Kenosha house. Eight men were expelled from the coach in short order, some heading to the privy, others to the station, all knowing this would be a longer stop than usual.

Reuben and Elly sat on a bench on the porch of the Kenosha House, watching as activity was picking up around the station. Several buckboards were coming down the road, loaded with folks that appeared to be ranching families from roundabout. A handful of riders were seen drawing near, and even a buggy was coming up the road from the direction of some of the gold camps. As they enjoyed watching the antics of the passengers and workers their attention was captured by a lone rider that came to the house, stepped down and stood a bit stiffly as he stretched his legs and bent backwards to stretch his back. Reuben watched, grinning. "What's the matter, Preacher, not used to ridin'?"

The rider looked to the man on the porch, broke into a grin and answered, "I'm not used to it, and it has tried my constitution, but I'm certain I will become accustomed to riding rather than walking. Thanks to some very dear friends that has made it possible! And I thank you, dear friends," he answered, giving an exaggerated bow as he doffed his hat and swung it to the side. He stood erect, smiling, and asked, "Are you staying for the preaching?"

"That's why we're here!" answered Reuben, standing, and motioning to the rocking chair beside them. The preacher nodded, smiling, and took a seat, slapping the arms and putting the rocker to the test. As he moved, several of the passengers started up the stairs, the gingham attired lady leading the way, the men following like a gaggle of moonstruck geese. As the woman came near, she nodded to the preacher and asked, "Are you the Itinerant Pastor?"

Preacher Dyer, stood, doffed his hat, and gave a slight nod, "Yes, ma'am, I am John Dyer, and I will be preaching shortly."

"We are looking forward to that, Pastor."

As the men filed past, two men, Jacob Binkley, and Abram Shoup, who had ridden with others, were talking rather animatedly and stepped to the side to continue their conversation before going inside. Binkley, attired more like a cowboy than a prospector, said, "That's right. Just in the last couple days, they've found three men dead, two up on Wilkerson Pass left alongside the trail, bodies mutilated, weapons gone, pockets rifled, and the boys at Hartsel's ranch are certain it was the same ones that killed James Addelman on his ranch by Ute Pass, cuz he was all cut up just like the other'ns."

Shoup nodded and began his own tale, "Well I heard about a couple killin's down Canon City way. A judge over by Hardscrabble was workin' at his sawmill and somebody gunned him down and left him lay, but not till after they split his head with an axe, cut out his heart and carved crosses on his chest. Nobody knows who dunnit, and then there was another'n o'er towards Fountain creek. A fella by the name of Henry Harkens, he was workin' his sawmill, and same thing. Shot dead, mutilated the same as the judge, and left where he fell."

"I didn't see 'em, but the fellas that found them up on the pass described the mutilations just like you said about the judge and that other fella. Head split, heart cut out and crosses carved on their chest," responded Binkley.

The preacher and Reuben could not help overhearing and the Preacher stood and walked closer to the men.

B.N. RUNDELL

"Overheard what you were saying about some men getting killed. They have any idea who was responsible?"

The cowboy Binkley answered, "Not that I know of, preacher. Coulda been just about anybody. Strange thing is most killin's like that are about robbery. But all three of these didn't have much of anythin' on 'em. Maybe a pistol or so, but no money nor gold, far as anybody could tell. And with the bodies left like they were, well . . ." looking away as he shrugged.

Shoup stepped closer. "Same thing with the two at the sawmills. The judge was known to be practically penniless, that's why he was workin' his sawmill. He was a good man, everybody liked him. No reason to it at all. But some o' those that been talkin' are sayin' it might be some Confederates, just killin' to be killin', others think it might be Injuns, but no scalps were taken, and there's the mutilations. It's plumb spooky is what it is," added Shoup. He had a small two by twice ranch and was bound for Denver City.

The preacher shook his head and motioned for everyone to go inside. "Service will start soon, so let's go inside, shall we?" he suggested. He walked to the far side of the large room usually used as the dining hall, but the table had been moved out and the chairs were arranged in rows, makeshift benches fashioned from split logs stood against the walls, and space for more to stand was allowed at the rear. Reuben and Elly chose one of the benches that had been carried in from the porch and was near the front. Several of the coach passengers crowded onto the far end of the bench and the crowd settled down when the preacher lifted his arms and said, "Let's begin by singing a hymn that is new to some, *Nearer My God to Thee*. I will sing it, the words are easy to remember, so join with me."

78

Nearer, my God to Thee, nearer to Thee.
E'en though it be a cross that raiseth me;
Still all my song shall be nearer, my God to
Thee.
Nearer my God, to Thee, nearer to Thee!

Everyone did their best to join in, stumbling over the words and most showed relief when he finished and motioned for everyone to be seated. "This morning, my message is on forgiveness. My text is taken from Psalm 86:5 *For thou, Lord, art good, and ready to forgive; and plenteous in mercy unto all them that call upon thee.* The words of the text say it all. God is ready to forgive, no matter the sin, or the sinner." The preacher continued about how everyone needs forgiveness and should also give forgiveness. He referenced several other passages, quoting most, and after about twenty minutes, he started to wrap things up as he said, "But the most important forgiveness is that forgiveness He gives when any sinner comes to Him in prayer seeking that free gift of salvation paid for by Jesus when He died on the cross for our sins. You see, my friend, no matter who we are, how bad or good we've been, there's only one way to Heaven and that is Jesus Christ and the gift of eternal life He offers to one and all. There must be a time in your life that you quit trying to make it on your own and give it all to Him. Has there been a time in your life that you have asked for His forgiveness and to receive that free gift of eternal life? If not, you can do so today, just bow your head and say something like this, *Father, forgive me my sins, come into my heart and save me by giving me that free gift of eternal life paid for by your Son, Jesus.* Remember, it's not the words you say, it's what you mean in your heart."

The preacher looked around the room, bowed his

head and spoke a prayer, asking God to guide each one to come to Him and ask for His forgiveness. He finished by asking God's blessing on each one present and closed in the name of Jesus. As he lifted his eyes, he noticed several were wiping tears away, others were restless and looking around, and the station keeper stood beside the preacher and announced, "Now if somebody will help with the table and chairs, we have breakfast of fresh deer steaks," he paused and nodded with a smile to Reuben, "vegetables and biscuits and gravy. Those of you on the stage have time, because your driver and messenger are takin' their time!"

Reuben and Elly stepped to the side, giving those with the stage first dibs on the meal because of the stage schedule. Another couple came to their side and the woman spoke to Elly, "Are you folks settling in the area?"

Elly smiled and walked with the woman out the door to find a seat on the porch, answering as they walked, "No ma'am, we're just passing through. We don't rightly know where we want to settle. For now, we're just enjoying the beautiful country."

As they moved away, the man of the couple offered his hand to Reuben, "Howdy, I'm Hamilton Case, we've got a little place east of here, up against the foothills."

"I'm Reuben Grundy, and the only place I have is between the pommel and cantle of my saddle!" he chuckled, shaking the man's hand.

"Passing through, are you? Or prospecting?"

"Passin', not prospectin'."

"After what those two fellas were sayin' before the service, passin' through might not be too safe."

"You mean those killings they were talking about?"

"Ummhumm, and add to that the Ute, Cheyenne, and

Arapaho Indians, not to dismiss the Confederates that also occasionally cause trouble."

"I understand, and it seems we've been up against a little bit of it all, except maybe the Utes, haven't run into them yet."

The rancher frowned and leaned back a little for a longer look at the tall young man before him, "What about the Arapaho and the Cheyenne and the Rebels?"

"Well, I spent a hitch with Berdan's Sharpshooters on the Union side, took a couple bullets that got me out. Run into the Cheyenne and did a little tradin' with Tall Bull, chief of the Dog Soldiers, then made friends with Little Raven of the Arapaho, he came to my weddin'. Ran into some more Confederates when I was workin' for Ben Holladay with the Overland Stage, but that wasn't much of anythin'."

The older man frowned, looking at Reuben and trying to determine if the young man was being truthful or was fooling him, then shook his head and walked away, obviously a little exasperated and doubtful of the truthfulness of such a young man. He motioned to his wife and nodded to their wagon, and she hustled off the porch to join her husband, turning to wave to Elly as they left.

Reuben watched the confused couple take to their wagon, the man mumbling and shaking his head as he slapped reins to the team, giving only a quick glance over his shoulder to the couple on the porch. Reuben grinned and waved, but the rattle of the door caught his attention as the two men that had spoken earlier came out of the station. "You fellas ridin' together?"

Binkley nodded. "Yup, since we're both goin' to Denver City, thought we'd ride together for the comp'ny."

"Well, after the stories you two told, I guess it goes without sayin' to watch each other's backs. Whoever it is that's doin' all that killin' must be almighty sneaky as well as dangerous."

"And you two as well. I'd hate to hear about anythin' like that happenin' to a pretty lady like you, ma'am," said Shoup, nodding and tipping his hat as he backed toward the steps.

Elly frowned, waited until the two men had mounted and left, and turned to Reuben. "Just what were you men talking about that was about killing?"

"I'll tell you later when we're back on the trail and away from here. Too many folks make me uncomfortable," answered Reuben, standing and starting toward the barn and their horses. As he moved to the barn, he was unaware that beyond a rolling hill that lay between the rising mountains behind the station and the stage road that came from Kenosha pass, sat two brothers, their horses tethered in the trees, watching the people leave the Kenosha House, their attention focused on those that traveled alone or with no more than two or three. They focused on the two men that took to the stage road that would take them over the pass on the way to Denver City, but they also watched the others, keeping in mind where each went and if they traveled alone.

13 / RED HILL

Mid-morning with the sun high in the clear blue sky saw Reuben and Elly moving south beside the stage road, preferring the untraveled soil to the hard pack of the roadway. Dotted with clusters of sage, cholla, prickly pear, rabbit brush, buffalo grass and creosote, the low rolling flats of South Park were anything but a garden of Eden. The most prominent color was dusty brown, what did not naturally show that color was coated with a thin layer of powdery dust from the brown clouds towed across the flats by the stagecoaches and other travelers. The rare patch of Indian paintbrush added a random touch of orange color that blended well with the yellow and magenta blossoms of the cholla. Prickly pear had already dropped their yellow blossoms, the thumb sized red pear that gave the plant its name showing itself at the end of each flat blade.

The usually talkative pair rode silently, pondering the recent events of the high-country flatlands. When Reuben related the stories of the grisly murders that had occurred, images of the dead at their own hands seemed to rise up to haunt their memories. Yet they were always vigilant and careful as they rode, knowing that even a few moments of careless inattention could result in their own deaths in this land where life was cheap, and the grim reaper rode a white horse with a sickle in his hand as he came uninvited and unwelcomed.

The mountains of the Mosquito range stood like hoary headed phantoms, watching over the travelers on the lonely stage road that split the park on its north/south passage. It took little imagination to think the mountains followed their progress, watching every move, bending, and twisting to keep them in view. But Reuben broke the dismal mood when he suggested, "How 'bout we go up the Tarryall? The preacher said there were a lot of diggin's up there and a couple towns with hotels and even an opera house!"

Elly smiled. "You mean there's a place where I can get a hot bath?" she chided, smiling at her man who was always anxious to see to her comforts and protection. He grinned at her, giving her the impression he had this side trip planned all along. They turned off the main stage road, taking the rougher and rutted road that sided Tarryall Creek, bound for the twin mining towns of Tarryall City and Hamilton.

"The preacher said the Massasoit Hotel in Tarryall, and Dunbar's in Hamilton were both good hotels, considerin' they were put up for prospectors and such. He said we'd probably want Dunbar's since there are more businesses in Hamilton and the Olympic Opera House is nearby."

"I don't much care about no opera house, unless they have something going on besides opera. But it might be nice to have a bath and a meal at a good restaurant," replied Elly, smiling as she twisted around in her saddle. They could see the burgeoning settlement that lay in the shadow of a timber topped finger ridge that was an offshoot of foothill ridges that lay at the base of granite tipped peaks of Boreas Mountain. Across the creek sprawled the smaller town of Tarryall City that pushed against the timbered skirt of Little Baldy Mountain.

All along the creek, prospectors were busy at rockers, sluice boxes, and a few were panning. As they neared the edge of the town, they heard the roar of several hydraulic mining operations blasting away at the creek banks and the nearby slopes. The noise of the hydraulics made the horses a little skittish, the mule moving to the far side away from the operations as Reuben moved farther away to draw nearer the town.

The long main street held a variety of businesses, mostly wood buildings, but some were false fronted tents. At the foremost end stood a large stable built by the Southern Stage Company, while down the street they could make out what appeared to be several boarding-houses, a hotel, many retail stores from general stores and emporiums to haberdashers and mining equipment, and almost every other business front was a saloon. As they neared the Dunbar hotel, they passed a recorder and a justice of the peace that shared an office. And everywhere there were people of all sorts; miners, prospectors, saloon keepers, gamblers, businessmen, and everything in between. Some old timers, long beards marred by tobacco stains, sat in rockers on the board-walk, watching and talking about everyone, a lop-eared dog sat beside the older man and only lifted one eyebrow as Elly passed with Bear on behind. A drunken man staggered into the street, trying to catch a noisy rooster that splashed through the mud and mire. A tinny piano banged away from one of the saloons and a stage-coach crowded its way to the stage station at the stables.

Three big freighters stood in front of the Hinckley and Company freighters office, apparently getting their final orders before departing for the supply point which was probably in Cañon City.

They checked in to the hotel, getting one of the last two available rooms, and as Elly made arrangements for a bath, Reuben trudged up the stairs to their room, dragging their bedrolls and haversacks, and would soon take the animals to the stables. After seeing beefsteak and potatoes as the special for the evening posted on the door, they had agreed that the restaurant off the lobby of the hotel would be more than suitable for their meal.

PREACHER DYER, AT THE INVITATION OF GEORGE Harriman, the owner and operator of the Kenosha House Stage station, had agreed to stay another day or two, and would be given the opportunity to preach each evening to the stage passengers and any other passersby. He sat on the porch watching the stage from Denver City coming to the station, the messenger was blowing his bugle to announce their arrival to the hostlers so they could have the next team ready to hook up. But this time was a little different, behind the stage were two saddle horses with what appeared to be bodies draped over the saddles. As the coach pulled up in front of the station, the preacher's assumptions proved correct as he saw two bodies, upper torsos wrapped in blankets, tied to the saddles.

He stood and went to the rail watching the driver shout out to the passengers, "Kenosha Station! All out for a stretch, meals if you want 'em and can pay for 'em!" The shotgunner went to the tied-off horses, unloosed them and led the animals with their gruesome burdens to the barn. The driver climbed the steps, saw the preacher and with a nod, explained, "We found them fellers just beyond the crest," nodding back toward the Kenosha Pass road, "one horse was standin' by his rider, the other'n trailin' his reins lookin' for graze. Both of 'em had their heads split open and were mutilated in other ways. Ain't never seen no Injuns do that before."

"Might not have been Indians. That one fella on the red dun was here just yesterday for the preaching and told us about some other murders just like that. One o'er by Hardscrabble, another'n by Fountain Creek, a couple atop Ute Pass and a rancher this side of Wilkerson Pass. All of 'em was cut up just like you said those two were." The preacher shook his head as he remembered the men, Jacob Binkley, and Abram Shoup, and how they had squirmed in their seats during his preaching but neither choosing to act on the words.

"You don't say! Then maybe it weren't no Injuns! But that makes it worse! If there's somebody goin' aroun' and killin' folks just to be killin' and nobody knows who they are, well . . . could be anybody!" declared the driver. He shrugged as he stepped through the door to follow the aroma of cooking food.

Preacher Dyer spent the rest of that day at the station, taking advantage of the opportunity to preach to a handful of passengers and several folks from a small wagon train loaded with mining equipment and big dreams. After a restless night, he rose early and had a quick breakfast with Harriman, and had an early start to the south, bound for the many mining towns that had sprung up in the past two years since the gold strike.

He moved southwest, taking the easy-going stage road. He passed the Tarryall Creek and wondered about his new friends, Reuben, and Elly, and if they had stopped at Hamilton or Tarryall City for a night in a hotel and a hot meal from a restaurant. He smiled as he thought of them, for they reminded him of his early days when he and his wife, Harriet Foster, began their life together and the many challenges they faced. But they were blessed with five children and the trials were well worth the reward, even though she had gone to glory almost fourteen years prior.

He had covered about dozen miles, moving at a leisurely pace, and crested the slight ridge that was known as Reinecker Ridge. The road skirted the flanks of the hill, but the black timber was edged by a wide band of quakies, and he decided to take his nooning in the shade of the beautiful white barked trees. He stepped down to a bed of matted leaves beside a little trickle of a spring fed stream, giving his horse a drink and rubbing him down with a handful of dry leaves. After loosening the girth, he took a package from his saddle bags that had been prepared by Harriman and smiled as he unwrapped the biscuits and bacon.

As he bit into the first cold biscuit, he thought some hot coffee would taste good, but he had neither the coffee nor the pot. He shook his head, grinning, and thought he would spend a little extra time in prayer as he let his horse graze and rest. Once finished with the biscuits, he rose and walked to the edge of the trees, looking down at the vast valley showing patches of brown but mostly green this early in the summer. A small patch of blue and white columbine grew near the quakies, and he took a moment to enjoy the beauty of God's handiwork. He started to word a prayer, but his attention was taken by the sound of gunshots. Two, no three, that sounded to the south. He stepped from the trees and walked to the edge of the rise, looking down the road to the distant razorback ridge that stretched like a skeletal finger from the foothills of Mount Silverheels pointing to the south end of the park.

He relaxed as he thought, *prob'ly some prospectors getting themselves some fresh venison. That Red Hill has always been good for deer and elk. Nothing to be concerned about.* But he returned to his mount and prepared to take to the trail. Always concerned about the many men that sat under his preaching and went about their daily work with no farther thoughts for the things of the Lord nor for their own eternity. *It could be someone signaling for help. Maybe he's hurt himself in an accident or something.* He stepped into the stirrup and reined the gelding around to ride the maybe three miles to Red Hill.

Stretching out to the south between the two ridges lay a green valley with the meandering Trout Creek coursing its way through the flats. Elk, mule deer, and antelope populated the land that would one day become prime cattle country. With the tall ridges siding the valley, it had yet to be ravaged by the gold hungry prospectors. Although a few prospect holes showed on the faces of the ridges, none had yielded color and the hopeful miners had moved into the hills where others had found their fortune.

Preacher Dyer angled across the face of the upper end of the long ridge, keeping to the well-traveled road used by both freighters and stages. The road took to a saddle crossing between a semi-bald bluff and a knob with the north facing slope black with thick timber. One tall spruce lifted its head high above the firs, spruce, and pines that covered the hillside. As the preacher started through the cut, he smelled the sickening stench of burning flesh. He reined up, pausing to look for smoke, and slowly nudged his mount forward. The horse tossed his head, his ears twitching back and forth as he bent around to look at his rider, questioning his choices.

As he neared the tree line, a thin wisp of smoke twisted its feathery tenacles through the leaves of the aspen seeking an escape from the confines of the forest. Preacher Dyer pushed the gelding into the trees toward the clearing and stopped short of the fire. Laying partially in the fire, the body of a decapitated man simmered in the coals, his head sitting on the nearby log, giving the appearance of watching the body burn. The preacher shook his head, muttering, *May God have mercy on their souls.* Realizing what he said, "their souls" he was reminded of the three shots he heard. He looked around the camp, two saddle horses stood picketed in the trees, nervously moving and stomping, trying the tethers as they bent their necks to look at the new visitor to the camp. With a quick glance around the camp, Preacher Dyer saw sign of two riders moving through the trees and followed. Just below the crest and lying sprawled in the middle of a patch of buffalo grass, lay another body. He looked around for any sign of the perpetrators and moved closer to the body. This one had his skull split, apparently like others that he had heard about. He knew these murders had happened less than an hour past, and he looked nervously around, then without any hesitation, he dug heels to the gelding, heading to Fairplay, the nearest town less than three miles away.

T he horse showed lather under the martingale, latigo, neck, and tail when Preacher Dyer brought it to a stop in front of the busiest place in town, Ma's Diner. As he swung down, a familiar voice said, "Say, Preacher, aren't you bein' a little hard on that horse? Looks like you run him all the way from Kenosha House!"

The preacher looked up as he slapped the rein around the hitchrail to see Reuben and Elly grinning as they watched. "Reuben, Elly! It's mighty good to see a friendly face!" he looked around at the many passersby, each one hurrying somewhere and no one getting anywhere, or so it seemed. "Have they got a sheriff here yet?" he asked.

Reuben frowned. "Not that I know of, but we've only been here since last night. Came in to find a place to stay, only room available was behind the restaurant here at Ma's boardin' house. Why? What's got you all fired up?"

Before he could answer two other men had stopped to greet the preacher, extending their hands as one asked, "Howdy Preacher Dyer! You gonna be holdin' meetin's soon?"

"Howdy, gentlemen. Yes, I will be holding meetings, but not here, up in Buckskin. But first I need to find some authority to report a couple murders!"

"Murders!?!" shouted the man, causing several others to crowd around and fire off questions. The preacher held up his hands. "Is there any authority, a sheriff or something?"

"Will I do, Preacher? I command the local company of volunteers for the territory. I'm Captain Lewis."

"That'll do. Now, I just found two fresh bodies up on Red Hill. Their horses are tethered at the campsite where one man was in the fire, the other'n is a little way down the hill in the brush. Both have been mutilated like the stories I've heard of the others." He shook his head and turned to Reuben, "Remember those two men that told us of the murders?"

"Yeah, the cowboy and the other fella, a drummer. What about 'em?"

"The stage found their bodies yesterday, just the day after we saw them at Kenosha House. They were mutilated also."

The captain stepped forward, "So, you know about the two the Denver stage reported?"

"Yes, they stopped at Kenosha House where I was staying and told us about them," replied the preacher.

The captain dropped his eyes, his hand cupping his chin, "Let's see now, that's seven, and with these two at Red Hill, that's nine killings!"

"That we know of, Captain," added Reuben, standing beside the preacher.

"Who are you?" asked the captain, suspicion showing on his face.

The preacher spoke up, "Oh, he's a friend of mine!

We came from Denver City and have been together all the while since."

The captain slowly lifted his head, then looked at the gathering and chattering crowd. He raised his voice, pointing at some men in the crowd, "Smitty! Hamhock! Short-stuff! . . . and you too, Jackson. You four men get your horses and weapons! You're coming with me!"

"Alright if I come along?" asked Reuben, looking at the captain.

"Fine by me, the more we have the better I'll feel about going out there!"

Reuben looked at a surprised Elly. "How 'bout you stayin' with the preacher, maybe buy him lunch? I think I need to ride along with these boys to see what we can find, cuz until these murderers are caught, it won't be safe for you'n me to be out on the trail by our lonesome!"

Elly smiled as she understood, reached for the preacher's arm, and smiled up at him and asked, "Would you like to have lunch with me?"

The preacher chuckled. "Yes'm, I'd be mighty honored to have lunch with you."

Reuben interjected, "I'll take care of your horse, Preacher. I've got to get Blue from the stables and I'll leave yours there."

"Thanks, Reuben, I appreciate that. And I'll take good care of Elly while you're gone!"

"Oh, I'm sure you will, Preacher. I *can* trust you, can't I?"

Both Elly and the preacher laughed as they started into the diner while Reuben took the preacher's horse and headed to the stables.

. . .

THE SIX MEN REASSEMBLED IN FRONT OF THE DINER WITH the captain giving the order to move out. He motioned for Reuben to join him at the front of the double column, and they rode from the bustling burg of Fairplay toward the long ridge known as Red Hill. "So, what brings you to Fairplay, gold?" asked the captain.

Reuben slowly shook his head, grinning. "No, Captain. My wife and I are just travelin' through the country. We've only been together less'n a year and we both wanted to see the mountains. After workin' a spell with Ben Holladay, we decided to take advantage of the time and opportunity and head west," explained Reuben, glancing sideways at the curious captain.

"What'd you do for Holladay?"

"Oh, just helped out with some shipments," replied Reuben, surprised at the captain's intrusive questions. It was kind of an unwritten way among men of the west that you didn't ask questions about a man's past. With so many trying to put the past behind them, some even taking new names, most kept their personal lives to themselves. He chuckled at the remembrance of talking to the postmaster at Hamilton who told him of the twenty thousand or so miners in the area, he guessed over four thousand had taken the name of Smith, requiring him to tell them to add a description so he would know them. Some added descriptions like, "Sam Smith, the husband of Hannah, father of six, who has a farm in Ohio next to the Alexanders."

Reuben looked at the captain and asked, "So, has anybody said who these murderers are, or what they look like?"

"No! And that's the frustrating part about the whole thing! Folks are suspicious of their own neighbors and most ever'body! That's why I was asking 'bout you.

'Course the preacher said you was with him, so I reckon you're not the one doing all this killing."

"Have you been charged with catchin' them?"

"Not particularly, but there's no other authority to speak of, no sheriff or nuthin', so . . ." he shrugged, glancing at Reuben. "But if you want the job, you're welcome to it!" he declared, his eyes showing a touch of hopefulness.

"Not me! I just got here and don't really have any plans of stayin'," declared Reuben.

The captain pointed at the bend in the road and started up the green slope that was mostly grass below the wide band of aspen. Near the crest of the hill, a long stretch of mixed pines showed as the backbone of the ridge. To their left, the long valley that fronted the Mosquito foothills stretched wide and long with the meandering appropriately named Crooked Creek keeping the bottom land green. A long stretch of red rimrock marked the crest, barely showing through the trees but occasionally showing their presence with the stacks of rocks jutting out as if pointing the way to the saddle crossing that folks were calling Red Hill pass.

"Preacher said they was in the trees so they shouldn't be too hard to find," stated the captain, standing in his stirrups to look through the trees.

Reuben cleared his voice to get the man's attention and when he turned, Reuben nodded just below the tree line near the scraggly skeleton of a long-dead aspen. The body of one of the men could easily be seen, crumpled in the grass. The captain looked. "Yeah, well, let's look for the other'n. And the preacher said their horses were here, so let's get them and put the bodies on the saddles."

Reuben nodded, looking to the saddle crossing and above the road to the trees. The road company had cut the stage and freight road from the side of the hill and the red soil had undercut the grass that held a tenuous grip as it overhung the cutaway. As the captain reined his horse to climb the bank, Reuben chose to follow the road. They met up at the camp, Reuben coming across the grassy flat, the captain working his way through the timber. As the captain broke from the trees, he saw Reuben first and said, "I saw the trail of the outlaws, heading thataway!" pointing along the ridge to the open flats of the park. Then his eyes settled on the remains of the victim and the captain lost his lunch. He leaned to the side and brought up everything he had eaten since before breakfast and he left a mess, coughing and spitting and wiping his mouth. The stench of burnt flesh still hung in the air, the pines and quakies holding it close. The captain reined his horse around and left the campsite in favor of the open air beyond the trees.

Reuben shook his head, stepped down and walked to the tethered horses, untying them and leading them closer to the body. He took the bedroll from behind the saddle and lay it on the ground, just as the other four men came into the campsite. Two had a similar reaction as the captain, but not quite as much and they also left the camp. The two that remained stepped down to help Reuben, one picking up the severed head, making a face that showed his disgust and held the head by the hair as he handed it to Reuben, his free hand covering his mouth and nose. He mumbled, "That's sick! Who would do such a thing?"

Reuben bundled the head together with the body in the blanket from the bedroll, bound the bundle with the leather thongs he cut from the man's saddle, and nodded to the man known as Jackson to help. The two men lifted the body to lay it across the saddle, tied it

THE TRAIL TO REVOLUTION

down, and led the horse away from the small pile of grey coals that marked their fire. The first man, Short-Stuff, whose name did not fit as he was three or four inches over six feet tall, but his slender frame, that would usually earn the nickname 'slim', apparently lost out to the contrasting nickname of Short-Stuff, climbed back aboard his mount, and took the reins from Reuben to lead the loaded horse from the trees. Reuben tossed the reins from the second horse to Jackson as he came near, then returned to Blue to mount up and follow.

While Jackson and Reuben loaded the second body, the captain and three others stayed in the shade of the aspen, watching the two work below. As they watched, a man came around the knoll, walking and carrying a pack, and upon seeing the men and the dead body, stopped, and stared. He looked from the two with the body to the others that had risen and were watching him, and immediately dropped his pack and took off running, eyes wide and arms pumping as he glanced back at the men, fear showing on his face.

The captain shouted at the others, "We need to get that man! He could be one of the killers!" Their horses had been picketed and given a chance to graze on the mountain grass, and the men had to get to them, tighten the girths, and mount up. The captain led them down to where Reuben and Jackson were finishing loading the second body. "That man's running like a guilty man!" He tossed the reins of the first loaded horse to Reuben. "You'n Jackson take these boys into town! We're going after that'n!"

Reuben frowned. "But, Captain, you saw the tracks. The killers were mounted and headed that way!" pointing to the southeast. The man on foot, now out of sight, had headed due south. "If you catch him, bring him back to town. At least give him a trial!"

"Yeah, yeah," shouted the captain, slapping legs to his mount to catch up with the other men.

Reuben stood watching the four leave, then turned to Jackson. "Is the captain always like that?"

"Whatdaya mean? Like what?"

"Anxious to take off after someone he knows nothing about. Jumpin' to conclusions."

"Yup. He's never been happy that the governor didn't make our volunteer unit a regular unit. He wanted to go fight in the war and didn't get a chance. Not yet, anyway."

"Oh, one of them, huh?"

"Ummhmm," replied Jackson, looking at Reuben with a bit of a frown. "You been in the war?"

"Ummhmm. Served my hitch with Berdan's Sharp-shooters."

"Blue or Grey?"

Reuben chuckled. "Green."

"Green?"

"Yup, our uniforms were green because we were on our own and had to sneak through the woods to do our job. We were Union troops," explained Reuben, grinning, but knowing there were plenty of the men in the gold-fields that had Southern sympathies.

15 / SUSPICION

The lone man staggered into the center of Front Street in Fairplay, no coat, no boots, dripping with sweat, waving his arms like a drunk but trying to cry out for help. The preacher and Elly had just come from the diner and saw the man, causing them to stop and look. The preacher quickly responded, running to the man, and catching him as he fell into his arms, the added burden taking them both to the ground. As he looked, the preacher recognized the man as John Foster, a man he knew from the times of preaching at California Gulch. He stood, lifting the man with him, and nodded to Elly as she motioned to the boarding house. The preacher helped the man, even though he heard someone in the crowd suggest, "Maybe he's the killer!?"

When they came to the front door of the boarding house, Elly opened it wide and directed the preacher to the room they had on the ground floor. As they entered, the man stumbled and the preacher helped him to a chair in the corner where the exhausted man, still struggling for breath, nodding, and tried to smile at the preacher.

Elly looked at the pair, shook her head, and asked, "Preacher, do you think it's safe to help this man? After all, he could be the killer."

The preacher grinned. "This man is not the killer. I know him from California Gulch. His name is John Foster, and he ran a 'Methodist Hotel' where preachers and believers were always welcome."

"Oh, well, then. Let's see if we can get him some coffee or a cup of tea," she suggested, leaving the room to the men. She had no sooner left the room and the front door opened to show Reuben enter. He smiled at Elly as she came into his arms, and they embraced. She pulled back, and explained, "The preacher is in our room with a man that came running into town, scared to death!"

Reuben frowned, looked at his woman, "You gettin' some coffee?"

"Ummhmm, wanna cup?"

"Sure do!" he answered as he started for the room.

The preacher was sitting on the edge of the bed, looking at the man, when Reuben walked in and asked, "So, what do we have here?"

"This is John Foster, a friend of mine from over in California Gulch."

Reuben nodded at the man, looked at the preacher and said, "We saw this man up on Red Hill and he took off runnin', so the captain and the others took off after him, leavin' Jackson and me to bring in the bodies you found."

"Is that right, John?" the preacher asked the weary looking wanderer.

"I thought they were the killers! They had a dead body they were puttin' on a horse and they looked at me like they were comin' after me! I took off and ran all the way here, by way of Trout Creek, up an' over the ridge a couple times, wadin' through the Middle Fork, and finally comin' into town!"

"It's a good thing you got away. I'm not sure what they would have done to you had they caught you. The captain said folks around here have been gettin' pretty jumpy and the two we brought in today aren't goin' to help matters none," offered Reuben, accepting a cup of coffee from Elly as she offered one to each of the men.

A knock at the door brought their attention to the doorway to see Jackson standing and looking at the man in the chair. He asked, "Is that . . .?" as he looked at Reuben.

"Ummhmm, that's him and he's not the killer. He's a friend of the preacher's who thought we were the killers!" chuckled Reuben, rising from the edge of the bed beside the preacher.

"Well, you better come out and explain it to the captain, he and the others are comin' into town now," suggested Jackson, stepping back from the doorway.

The two men walked through the narrow alleyway beside the diner to step onto the boardwalk in front of the businesses. As they walked, Jackson looked to Reuben. "Those two we brought in? Somebody recognized them. Seems they were miners from over California Gulch way named Frederick Lehman and Sol Seyga." Reuben nodded, watching as the captain and the three others rode into town on tired horses showing dried lather. The men sat hung shouldered, heads hanging, until Jackson called out, "Hey, Captain! Glad you made it back. Where's your prisoner?" he chided, grinning.

The captain frowned, looked at Jackson and suspected something from the man's actions and asked, "Why?"

"Cuz he already came into town and is enjoyin' a cup o' coffee o'er at Ma's boardin' house with the Preacher!"

The captain scowled, looking from Jackson to Reuben, "What?" he asked, knowing there was more to the tale.

Reuben spoke up, "Seems he's not the killer after all. He's a friend of the preacher's from over California Gulch way and he thought we were the killers. That's why he ran, after all, we're the ones that had the dead bodies!"

The captain nudged his mount to the hitchrail and stepped down. He tied off his horse, mounted the steps to the boardwalk and started for the diner when a rider came near and leaned on his pommel as he called out to the captain, "Hey, Captain! There's a man hidin' out o'er toward Tarryall Creek, that ranch that's in the valley there. The man I talked to said he thought it was one o' them killers!"

The captain looked at Jackson. "Take my horse to the stables, get me a fresh mount; you too. We're going after this'n. I'll get Ma to pack us some grub, you tell the others, an' see if you can get some more of the men." Jackson turned and with the rein of the captain's mount in hand, trotted up the street to the stables. The captain turned to Reuben. "You coming?"

"Nah, I think I'll sit this one out. Can't be leavin' my wife with the preacher too often, folks'll start talkin'!" he chuckled.

It was late the next day when the line of bedraggled men rode into town, horses' heads hanging, feet dragging, and men dusty, and weary. The setting sun shone bright against their faces, casting an eerie glow of orange across the town and the men. Their heads hung low, chins bouncing on their chests, sweat leaving trails through the dust on their faces, and none looking at the many folks watching them return. When they neared, Reuben called out to Jackson, "Hey, Jackson!"

The man turned to look, and Reuben stepped closer. "How 'bout me buyin' you some supper?"

Jackson turned to look at the captain and the others, none of whom were looking at him or Reuben, and he nudged his horse to the hitchrail in front of Ma's Diner and wearily stepped down. He went to the water trough, followed by Reuben who pumped the handle for him to put his head under the water. The man let the water run over his head and neck, splashing more on his face and chest, then stood, hands on the edge of the trough and shook off the excess. He lifted his head to look at Reuben, nodded for him to lead the way and followed his new friend into the diner. Elly and the preacher were already seated at a table in the corner by the window, and Reuben and Jackson joined them.

As they sat down, the waitress filled their cups with steaming coffee, looked at Reuben and Jackson and asked, "Specials?"

"That'll be fine, thanks," said Reuben and watched as the middle-aged woman with premature grey hair walk away toward the kitchen.

Reuben turned to Jackson. "So, looks like you and that bunch were worn out!"

Jackson shook his head. "That ain't the half of it!" and with a glance around the room, that was mostly empty since it was a little after the usual supper time, began to tell his story.

"There was a man holed up at the ranch alright, just like that fella said, and when we got there, close to sundown, the captain demanded they surrender the man. But the rancher refused no matter what the captain said, so we decided to wait 'em out." Jackson paused, took a big sip of hot coffee, and after a deep breath, he leaned his elbows on the table and drew close so he could speak in low tones.

"In the night, the captain was thinkin' 'bout chargin' the house, but someone shot at us and hit the mule! Killed him! And that made the captain mad, but we convinced him to wait till mornin'." Another pause and another sip and he continued. "Come mornin', the captain said, 'If you don't surrender that man, we'll burn your house down around you!' Now that surprised all of us, but we figgered the captain was bluffin' and the man inside hollered out that we could have the man. So, the captain and Smitty and Short-Stuff went in, and the captain demanded the rancher give up a horse or a mule to pay for the one he shot, so the rancher did. Then here come the captain and Smitty, the fella between them." Jackson paused, shook his head as he finished his coffee and sat the cup down. He looked around the table at each one, "Then we started back to town, but when we got to Trout Creek, we stopped to water the horses, and the captain, he walked around lookin' at things and came back and said, 'This is as good a place as any. There's a big cottonwood yonder with a sturdy limb that'll do just fine.'" Jackson shook his head again, looking into his empty cup at the dregs, then lifted his eyes to each one, "And then we hung him!"

The preacher was aghast, looked from Jackson to Reuben, and back to Jackson. "You hung him? Well, surely you had a trial or something?"

"Nope. The captain said, 'The other'n got away, this one ain't! We'll hang him right here! It's time we made this valley safe again!' and then ordered us all to do the deed. No man said anythin', I think we all were afraid to buck him. He can be fearsome when he's crossed!"

Reuben dropped his eyes to his cup, slowly shaking his head, glanced at the preacher and to Elly who gave him a look of askance, but he gave her the sign to remain quiet. Although he still carried the badge, he wasn't sure if it carried any authority, and he did not want to insert himself in local issues. The captain was the closest the town had to any lawman, and what had been done could not be changed. Perhaps it *would* give the people some reassurance that they did have some protection against the killers.

The foursome ate their meal with little conversation, each one mulling the account of the hanging. As they neared the end of the apple pie, the preacher commented, "I think I'll be heading to Buckskin in the morning. I promised folks there I would hold some meetings and I believe I am needed at a time like this."

"Preacher, a man of God is always needed, but especially at a time like this," replied Reuben with a glance at Elly. "And if you don't mind, how 'bout we ride along with you. I've heard good things about the settlements up thataway and we'd kinda like to see 'em."

The preacher smiled, nodding. "I would be grateful for the company!"

T he rising sun was at their backs and cast a rosy glow on the mountains round about, making long shadows of the trees beside the trail pointing their way to penetrate deep into the towering mountains. Elly let Bear run beside her Appy, keeping watch on him as he sniffed at every bush, tried to mark each one, and still keep up with the group. This was his first time to run free and she marveled at the rambunctious pup and his endless energy. Looking more like a wolf than her pup, she grinned as he bounced along, tail wagging and tongue lolling.

Preacher pointed to the tall peak off their right shoulder that caught and held the golden glow of the rising sun. "See that peak there? That's Mount Silverheels. Ever hear the story about that?"

"Can't say as we have, Preacher," responded Reuben, looking at the mountain that rose high above timberline, its granite peak hoarding the remnants of the past winter's snowfall.

"Seems there was a time, little over a year ago, when the stage brought a woman to town that was outfitted in a fine dress and veil, and to everyone's surprise, she no sooner stepped off the stage that she walked into Billy Buck's saloon and asked for a job, dancing and entertaining. Now she wasn't the typical dance hall girl, she was a talented and trained dancer, and folks said she was mighty beautiful. She always wore a fine pair of shiny shoes, all sparkly and such, and folks naturally called her Silverheels. She had her a cabin across the creek and walked to work ever' evening."

Then one day a couple Mexican sheepherders brought a flock o' sheep to town to sell to the restaurants and hotels. What folks didn't know was they had smallpox! Well, the plague quickly spread, and men were falling sick left and right, no one to care for 'em. So Silverheels started going from cabin to cabin to tent and such, tending to the sick men. She kept at it for weeks and nursed many of 'em through the pox. But 'fore long, she took the pox herself. But the men were so grateful for what she done, a bunch of 'em got together, took up a collection, and were going to give it to her. They went to the cabin, and she was gone! They never did know what happened to her, but in memory of what she done, they named that mountain after her, Mount Silverheels!"

The preacher had just finished his story when they moved to the side of the road to let pass a man driving a team of oxen pulling a wagonload of lumber. They nodded to one another, and the preacher greeted him, "Morning, Mr. Metcalf."

"Mornin', Preacher Dyer," responded the man, tipping his hat as he looked at Elly.

The preacher explained, "That's probably from the sawmill at Buckskin. Only one around this area now."

Buckskin was about seven to eight miles from Fairplay and off the main stage road that was being built to

Breckenridge. Although a couple of early settlers and miners had changed the name to Laurette to honor their wives, most still called it Buckskin. They took the road that mounted the shoulder of a long finger ridge and cut through the black timber. As they rounded the knob at the end of the ridge, the valley that stretched to the west and cut between the towering mountains of the Mosquito range, showed itself to be a bastion of activity that stretched on both sides of the creek all the way past the huge talus slope on the flanks of the big mountain to bend around to the north and out of sight.

Buildings and tents were scattered on both sides of the creek with most on the north side pushing up against the stumps and trees that had given way to the determined prospectors. The obvious main street showed several wooden buildings rising to two stories and crowded together. The preacher pointed out a gambling hall near the end of Front Street. "First time I held services here, that gambling hall was the only space available. But folks came and we had a good meeting!" He shook his head, grinning, "And even with all the opposition, they've asked me to hold more meetings."

"Opposition?" asked Elly, frowning as she looked at Dyer.

"Aside from the usual, gambling halls, saloons, and such, there's Professor Fornia's dancing institute, a theater, two dance halls, and more. But the Lord's work must be done!" he declared, nudging his mount forward.

As they rode through the town, Reuben and Elly noted a bank with a sign declaring *Dealers in Gold Dust, Coin, and Exchange,* and were surprised to see four hotels, The Laurette, Pacific House, Cherokee, and the O.K. House. The saloons were too numerous to count, but they also saw the Drug and Yankee Notion Store and

Kitchen's General Store. Preacher had told them the town had quite a notorious reputation and had more folks involved in the various businesses, both reputable and questionable, as there were men in the mines.

The preacher twisted around in his saddle to look at Reuben and Elly, "I recommend the Pacific House for a hotel. They have clean rooms and a decent café. I have friends I'll be staying with, but I'd like to meet you for lunch, if you'd like?"

"That'd be fine, Preacher. We'll get us a room, get settled in and put the animals up, then we'll meet in the café."

The preacher nodded and reined his mount to a cross street that led to an area with several houses and tents. Reuben looked at Elly. "What do you think of this boom town?"

"Honestly, after seeing Hamilton, Tarryall, and Fairplay, I'm kinda tired of boom towns and all these people. I thought we were gonna be exploring mountains where there was nothing but beautiful country and you and me!"

"Well, you know I'm a little concerned about these killings goin' on, and not knowin' how much we're expected to do, you know, carryin' these badges and all," explained Reuben.

"Those appointments were more for the gold shipments and the Confederates. I didn't think they were as regular deputy marshals. But I s'pose you could wire the governor and see what he has to say about it," suggested Elly as they walked into the hotel.

"Welcome, folks!" greeted a cheerful young man. The clerk looked to be barely out of his teens, wavy dark red hair, and an abundance of freckles. His broad smile showed pearly whites and his eyes danced with mischief.

A string tie hung from his starched collar that topped a striped cotton shirt tucked into corded trousers. "Thanks for coming to the Pacific Hotel, where we will do anything to make your stay enjoyable! Would you like a room for one night or more?"

Reuben stepped to the counter, grinning, and looked at the young man. "We're not sure. But we'll let you know before we check out, how's that?"

"That will be fine, sir, ma'am," as he glanced to Elly. He spun the registration ledger around for Reuben to sign and turned away to fetch a key for the room. As Reuben finished signing, the young man looked at the name, "Mr. and Mrs. Reuben Grundy, welcome. Your room will be number twenty-six, second floor front, with a view of the town. Will there be anything else?"

"Yes, I'd like a bath, please," said Elly, lifting her bedroll to her shoulder as Reuben picked up the haversacks and saddle bags.

"Yes, ma'am. I'll have the maid draw you a bath and the bathing room is just down the hall from your room. It will be ready shortly; the maid will rap on your door to let you know."

"Thank you," said Elly, tossing the words over her shoulder as she started up the stairs.

REUBEN STOOD AS HE SAW THE PREACHER COME THROUGH the doorway to the dining room and motioned to the man to join them. He was surprised to see a couple with him and quickly looked around for an additional chair to accommodate the pair. As the broad smiling preacher neared, he glanced from Reuben to Elly and then turned slightly. "Reuben, Elly, these are my good friends, Horace and Augusta Tabor. Folks, this is Reuben and Elly Grundy, also good friends."

Reuben stretched out his hand to Horace, nodding to his wife, Augusta. "Good to meet you, folks, join us, please," and motioned to the three chairs around the edge of the round table.

"And it's a pleasure to make your acquaintance, Reuben, Elly," said Horace. Augusta added, "It certainly is, and welcome to our community. It's always good to see new faces here."

The two spoke as they seated themselves beside the preacher and once settled, looked at the new couple. "The preacher says you're just traveling through and are not looking for a rich gold strike. Now that makes you the exception around here, for if they're not digging for gold, they're mining for it in other ways!" stated the man. Horace was what some would call 'portly' with a bit of a paunch held in by a tight fitting but well-tailored brocade vest. His frock coat hung beside the seat, the tall collar standing stiff behind the starched white collar of his linen shirt. His string tie hung loosely, but the pearl buttons showed opulence.

Augusta wore a simple dress of pin striped linen, the long line of buttons was closely set and angled from the waist to the shoulder. The dress was surprisingly form fitting, and she was sans hoop that was the usual fashion. She had a lace stole and a matching lace cap. Her hair was parted in the middle, pulled tightly to the side, and ended in curls that framed her face. She was not a beautiful woman, but certainly not unattractive. She looked at Elly, smiling, and said, "Perhaps we ladies need to have some time to ourselves in the coming days. Would that be alright?"

"That would be fine, and I would enjoy the company

of a woman for a change. However, I'm not certain how long we will be here," she added, glancing to Reuben.

The small talk continued, interrupted briefly by the waitress to take the orders, and fill their coffee cups. As she left, the diners were interrupted by a man at the door, "Folks! May I have your attention, please?"

The chatter subsided, several turned their chairs to look to the intrusion, and the man continued, "Folks, some of you may know me, I'm Harold Stansell of the bank. Now as most of you know there have been some grisly murders happening throughout our area, from Wilkerson Pass to Kenosha Pass and other places. Now they struck near here. Some of you may know Frederick Carter, a miner with a claim west of here. He was killed as he was going to Fairplay just this morning." He paused as folks murmured their surprise, looking to one another. "While they were doing their grisly work, Edward Metcalf, the sawyer from here in Buckskin was taking a load of lumber to Fairplay and was shot at, but fortunately his oxen stampeded and although a bullet had struck his chest, his papers, Bible and more saved his life. But he is the first to see the killers and gave a good description of them." He paused again and several started asking questions and talking among themselves. Elly looked at Reuben, knowing what he was thinking and slowly shook her head. The banker raised his hands for silence and continued, "Because two of the victims were from over by California Gulch, and others known by folks around here, there is a posse forming and we're looking for men that could take a few days and help track down these killers once and for all! Now John McCannon is outside talking to men now, and if you are interested in joining, please see him right away."

Reuben turned to Elly, speaking softly, "You know I

can't sit back and let them hang another innocent man. If these are the killers, they must be caught."

"But what about the governor?" asked Elly.

"You send the telegram, a copy to Holladay, and I'll go with these men. If the authority is needed, well, I'll give it. But . . ." he shook his head, remembering Jackson's telling of the hanging and knowing if he had gone with them, he might have prevented it. He leaned over, kissed her, and stood to leave. "If you folks will excuse me?" and walked away.

"**F**elipe! You missed! Should we go after him?" declared a flabbergasted Vivián, looking at his brother with disbelief.

Felipe had been surprised when the man on the lumber wagon came down the road. Anyone else would have paid little attention to two men and horses in the tall willows, but oxen plod along, and the driver was constantly looking around. When Felipe saw the man looking, he grabbed up his rifle and snapped off a shot, knowing he hit the man, but he didn't fall. The rifle shot and the scream of the driver startled the oxen and they stampeded. Felipe fired again and missed again, prompting him to shout and scream curses after the man on the wagon.

Felipe stood, looking down on the headless corpse before him, the heart of the man lay in a puddle of blood to the side, a crucifix carved on his chest, and Felipe looked up at his younger brother, Vivián José Espinosa. "We cannot go to Buckskin or the diggings up the gulch. We must leave this area quickly!" He went to the little creek to wash off the blood and to wipe his knife clean.

Vivián was already splashing in the water, the head of the man sitting on the bank beside him as if watching his murderer clean himself. Felipe rose and walked behind his brother and kicked the head into the water. *"Vamos rápido!"*

Felipe swung into his saddle, digging his big rowel spurs into the horse's ribs and with a glance to his brother who had put one boot into the tapaderos, he took to the trees. A shout from Vivián told of his frustrations with his skittish horse, as his horse, anxious to follow Felipe's mount, was kicking dirt as he scampered into the trees, Vivián holding onto the saddle horn, one foot dragging, the other stuffed deep into the tapadero. Felipe laughed at his brother but knew he would overcome his frisky horse and quickly join him. They had been in the trees and willows by the creek south of the road, but with a quick glance up and down the road, he raced his mount across and into the trees at the base of the long, timber-covered ridge.

They kept to the trees, slowing their movements to lessen the sounds of their passing, crested the ridge and dropped to the west side, going to the edge of the trees, and stopping. The horses' sides were heaving, and Felipe showed unusual concern for his Andalusian bred stallion by reaching down and stroking his neck and speaking to him. It was just shy of midday and most of those using the road in the heat of the day were freighters and none appeared. He motioned to his brother and stared across the flats west of the circuitous middle fork of the South Platte. They were a little over a mile above the fork in the road that led to Buckskin and few travelers used this road which would lead to Breckenridge.

They pushed through the willows, crossed the shallow river, and were slowed by the marshland thick with cattails and mud. The horses sloshed about, the mud sucking at their hooves with each step, but soon struck solid ground and took to the trees of the long ridge that sided the river as it flowed south. The west side of the slope was thick with black timber, but a game trail can usually be found in the thick woods, as the deer and elk must also pass through and would choose the easiest way. Felipe pointed his mount onto a thin trail, as they quietly moved across the pine needle carpeted path. He thought about the man that fled on his lumber wagon, wondering if he had a very good look at him and his brother. Whether he could tell anyone what they looked like was of little concern but putting someone on their trail did worry Felipe.

He paused to look around at the contour of land on which they traveled. Surrounded by black timber thick with spruce and fir, he twisted around, bent side to side, searching for other game trails or breaks in the timber. He turned away from the trail and picked his own way through the trees, dodging limbs, pushing aside branches, laying low on his horse's neck, and with daylight his goal, they soon crested the ridge. Breaking from the trees, he saw a wide and long mountain meadow, long grass waving in the breeze, bright sun showing the patchwork of grasses and sedge. As they moved into the open, Felipe stood in his stirrups to look to the east and the end of the meadow, saw that it pointed to a shoulder that dropped back into the valley of the South Platte. Another knoll promised cover of timber and another draw farther east that beckoned. He nodded toward the bigger knoll, glanced at his brother, and kicked his horse to a canter to cross with wide open meadow.

The northern end of the knoll offered a saddle

crossing and Felipe slowed, and quickly made his decision to cross over, hoping the far side would give ample cover and a way out of these mountains. Vivián came alongside, "Felipe, are we going back to *nuestra casa*?" He had a hopeful look on his face until Felipe glowered and answered, "We have no home. The Anglos destroyed everything!"

Vivián hung his head, remembering his family and the way the soldiers destroyed their home and his family. He had killed only one before he fled, but it was that lust for blood and vengeance that drove him to kill. He looked at the creek in the bottom of the long draw. "But we go south, yes?"

"*Si, si.* We go south," replied a very tired Felipe as he dug spurs to his mount.

————

"But, Reuben! We've fought Cheyenne Dog Soldiers, hold-up men, renegades, and Confederates together, so why can't we be together on this hunt?" pleaded Elly, anxious to be by her man's side instead of staying in a hotel and socializing with women and a preacher.

Reuben drew her close, looked down into her upturned face, smiled and said, "This is different."

"How? How is it different?" she asked, staying close and keeping her eyes on his.

"Because with all the others, most of the fightin' was with rifles while we were behind cover, and it was easy to tell the good from the bad. Now, just like the bunch that hung that fella the other day, the good can turn bad faster'n an eagle can catch a whistle pig! There will be prob'ly a dozen men in the posse, all of 'em full of blood lust and wantin' to be the one to drop a hammer on the killers. I won't be surprised to see some of 'em fall to their own guns! No, it's just too uncertain, especially if we put a beautiful blonde woman in the middle of a dozen dirty miners and wannabe soldiers, there's no tellin' how crazy some of 'em might get! No. I won't have it!"

She smiled up at him, snuggled a little closer. "You think I'm a beautiful blonde woman?" she purred.

He chuckled, cocked his head to the side and whispered into her ear, "And that's not all I'm thinkin'!" he declared as he gave her a long kiss.

As she pulled back, she looked up at him smiling, "Oh, all right. I'll stay here and try to act like a lady. I'll send that telegram for you, but you better hurry back to me, safe and sound, y'hear?"

Reuben smiled, gave her another peck on the lips and said, "Don't forget that telegram, and a copy to Holladay. I might come back with these fellas all under arrest and I need to know I have full authority if that's necessary!"

She nodded and stepped back, gaining the shade from the overhanging balcony of the hotel. They stood on the boardwalk and Reuben turned back to Blue to tie on the saddle bags and put his bedroll on behind the cantle. Several other men had returned to the front of the hotel, looking for John McCannon and the rest of the posse.

Three men walked beside McCannon, all leading their horses as they came to the hotel. McCannon stepped onto the boardwalk, looking around at the four men who stood waiting, and addressed the men, "Men, the word I got was Mr. Metcalf said there were two men, he thought they were Mexicans because of the way they were dressed, both were dark skinned, and one had a white sombrero. He thought the other one also had a sombrero hanging at his back. He doesn't know what their horses were, or anything else. He said he was too scared and almost left the wagon behind cuz he thought he could outrun 'em on foot!" The waiting men laughed at the image of the man trying to outrun his own wagon but looked back to McCannon for more. He continued, "I don't know how long we're gonna be out, but I'm thinking we need to do what we can to catch these devils!" The men nodded, cheered, and shouted, "Hear, hear!"

"First, we need to elect a captain, someone to lead this posse."

The man beside Reuben spoke up, "What about you, John?"

"Yeah! Let's have McCannon be the captain," shouted another.

"Well, it doesn't have to be me, anyone can do it," added John.

"All in favor of John say aye!" shouted one man standing beside his horse.

The crowd of men shouted "Aye!" and no one dissented.

McCannon nodded and said, "Then let's get at it!" and stepped off the boardwalk to climb into his saddle. He pulled his horse's head around and started off down the street as the rest of the posse clamored to get aboard and follow. Within moments, they were out of town and lined out by twos and threes, staying on the road until they came to the site of the killing. McCannon stopped, stepped down and walked closer to the willows, looking for sign of the killing and spotted bloody grasses and lifted his hand to tell the others he found it. He hollered,

"Hey, Foley! You're a tracker, come find where they pulled out!"

A whiskery man wearing a buckskin jacket and whip-cord trousers swung his leg over his pommel, slid to the ground and padded in his moccasins to McCannon's side. Reuben watched the wiry older man, guessing him to be in his early fifties, and chuckled as he spat tobacco from his toothless mouth, much of it coursing through his whiskers. His bow legs cut through the tall grass as he waved his hands across the top of the grasses squinted and stepped lightly toward the trees. He turned back to the captain., "They went thataway!" pointing to the trees.

Reuben bent down and grabbed the reins to Foley's mount and started into the willows, the others following, one leading McCannon's mount, and handed off the horse to the wily old mountain man. With McCannon leading, Reuben and Foley behind, the posse took to the trees, following the sign of the killers, hopeful of making this a short and fruitful chase, but only time would tell.

18 / SEARCH

"I 'm tellin' ya, they musta sprouted wings an' flew o'er this mud and 'dobe!" declared Foley. He and Reuben had been chosen to scout the trail ahead of the others and they now stood beside their mounts, overlooking the mud flats that carried Four Mile Creek from the high mountains.

"I reckon we got so used to followin' their trail with little effort, they slipped out from under us," offered Reuben. He sat down on the edge of the slight bank, elbows on his knees and looked around. Foley joined him and waited, reading the sign of someone thinking things through. "Let's see, they headed east outta Buckskin, crossed the Middle Fork of the South Platte, went over the ridge, still goin' east. Then they turned south, crossed the ridge above Fairplay, and angled off to the west, but still goin' mostly south, to here." He looked around, a long searching gaze of the flats of South Park, looking directly south along the foothills of the Mosquito Range, and another lingering look at the dark line of timbered foothills that bordered the south end of South Park.

He looked to Foley, frowned. "Is Wilkerson Pass, Ute Pass, down at the southeast end of the Park?"

"Uh, yeah, it's o'er that direction. Where you goin' with this?"

"And is Hardscrabble farther south?"

"It is. Quite a ways beyond Cañon City toward the Sangre de Cristos."

"I think they're retracin' their route. They came from there, and they're goin' back!" declared Reuben, standing. He went to his saddlebags and withdrew the binoculars for a better survey of the valley. Rejoining Foley at the edge of the slope, he resumed his position with knees drawn up and elbows supported. He searched the valley for any obvious sign in any direction, but the only life he saw was a distant band of Pronghorns and two slow-moving prospectors leading burros toward the goldfields behind them. "Nothin'!"

"Then we better report back to the others. The sun's tryin' its darndest to slip behind them there mountains an' it'll be dark soon. How 'bout you checkin' that little oasis of trees yonder, find us a campsite?"

"Sounds good to me. Might even get a fire goin' for coffee!"

"Ain't nuthin' can make me get a move on like the smell of fresh coffee!" chuckled Foley, swinging aboard his mount and pulling his head around to start back to fetch the others.

Reuben laughed as he watched Foley leave, then stepped aboard Blue to move toward the island of green that sat beside the little creek. Tall ponderosa blended with cottonwoods and promised a decent site for the night. As he neared the trees, he jumped a mule deer buck and was quick about drawing the Henry from the scabbard and taking a narrow bead to drop the buck as he cleared the willows. Reuben smiled, knowing everyone would be glad to have some fresh meat, even though this was the first night on the trail, for a hearty meal would make everyone feel good about their progress.

COME EARLY MORNING, THE BLUSH OF GOLD LAY LIKE A billowy blanket on the eastern horizon while the golden lances gilded the edges of the few lazy lingering clouds. John McCannon summoned the men of the posse together around the morning fire, each one holding their steaming cup of coffee close and sipping on the black brew. "Men, our scouts have reported the loss of the tracks of the killers. Last place there was any sign, was out yonder," pointing into the wide basin of South Park, where the Middle Fork of the South Platte sided the tail end of Red Hill, "So, we'll be sending out three scouts. That'll be Reuben and Foley, who'll go south and swing along the foothills to see if they can cut any sign of 'em." He paused, looking around the group of manhunters. "We had a few more men join us from Fairplay an' Breckenridge. So, Charles Carter, you and J.A. Spaulding there, I want you fellas to ride this side of Red Hill, then cut east to the Puma Hills and head south. We wanna cut any sign of 'em leaving the park."

McCannon looked around again, nodded to two men standing side by side. "Youngh, you take Joe Lamb with you and go straight east across the tail end of Red Hill, cross on over Trout Creek and that serrated ridge yonder, and ride those rolling hills south to the foothills where you'll prob'ly meet up with Reuben and Foley."

Satisfied with his choices, he refilled his coffee cup, looking around at the others that seemed to be awaiting instructions. "Doc Bell said they heard about a couple suspicious men that were said to be hanging out up by Tarryall and they left of a sudden like, heading our direction. Now you scouts," nodding to the second and third group of chosen scouts, "you keep close watch 'cuz those two might be the same ones we been tracking. But the rest of us are gonna head thataway to see if we can find those other two, just in case.

"We'll all meet up tomorrow night at the foot of Three-mile Mountain. First one there's gotta have supper going! Now, let's get some tucker under our belts and get on the trail!"

The sun was laying low on the eastern hills, giving a golden glow to the few clouds stretched across the big sky, when the posse divided and went their separate ways. McCannon took the point of the cavalcade with Dr. Bell at his side, as his group started back to the north, hoping to find the two characters from the Tarryall area. The three pair of scouts split up and pointed their horses into the rising sun. Reuben looked to Foley. "McCannon seems to know what he's doin'. You known him long?"

"Nah, never talked to him 'fore. Seen him around the saloons and café e'er now an' then, but he's more of a miner, while I'm not after the gold but do a little huntin' for folks. But I ain't heared nuthin' bad about him. Why?"

"Oh, just wonderin'. There was some volunteer recruits back to Fairplay that caught up with a fella, wasn't one of the killers, and 'fore they got back to town, they hung him!"

Foley frowned, twisted around in his seat to look at Reuben. "Was he guilty of somethin'?"

"Only thing he was guilty of was gettin' caught. That's

why I was wonderin' about McCannon. Don't want somethin' like that happenin' again, leastways not while I'm around."

Foley turned back around in his saddle, shaking his head and mumbling, until Reuben asked, "What are you grumblin' about?"

"I ain't never been nuthin' but a hunter! An' I've gone up against Ol' Ephraim, *that's a grizzly bear to you*, black bear momma with her cubs helpin', a bull moose that charged from a lily pond, and a whole herd o' buffalo. An' I ain't never had to hunt down a man 'til now! And if'n that's the way they're gonna be, what's to keep 'em from hangin' each other?" He shook his head, doffed his hat and wiped his brow and looked sideways at Reuben, then spat, "People! Gimme a grizz ever time! At least you know where you stand with ol' Ephraim. He looks at you 'cuz he's thinkin' how you'd taste and if you're worth the effort, or maybe too tough to chew. But they don't lie to you, they come straight at'chu, an' if'n you win out, at least you got yourself a warm coat for the winter! Tain't so with people."

Foley chuckled, grinned at Reuben. "An' that's the longest I preached in a long time!"

Both men laughed, and Reuben allowed his mind to consider what his new friend had said, simple terms though they were, for often the most profound truths are found in simple thoughts.

"You know, Jim, from what I've seen, it's not the purpose men set themselves to, but the things that happen along the way. Take for example, those men that hung that fella. From what I knew about those that went after him, they sincerely meant to capture a murderer and protect their family and friends from any farther killin's. But," and he paused, searching for words, "whenever some folks get a little power, become the one to make the decisions, that might be the first time they've been involved in somethin' that important and the power goes to their head and they forget about their accountability to the people. That's when they think they can do anythin' and not have to face the consequences, because, after all, they are the ones in charge and are required to make the difficult decisions. Yet all too often, they don't think out what they're doing, they just act, and then others end up payin' for their foolishness."

They rode in silence for a while until Foley turned to look at Reuben again. "Were you in the war?"

"Ummhumm."

"So, you seen it firsthand, huh? Men that shoulda still been plowin' fields and instead put on a fancy uniform and orderin' men around, even though they don't know them own selves just what they were doin'. Yeppir, seen it myself! Too many times! Some popinjay from the city that belonged behind a counter of a woman's corset store, out in front like he knew what he was doin'!" declared the grisly old hunter, shaking his head.

Reuben chuckled, nodded, and looked to the trail ahead. They broke for nooning and found shade in a thick grove of aspen, until they heard the shuffling footfalls of many ridden horses, moving through the trees higher up the slope from where they lazed. Blue lifted his head, ears pricked and nostrils flaring, looking into the deeper darkness of the thick pines, before turning to look at Reuben as he came alongside to slip the Henry from the scabbard at his side.

19 / UTE

Kaniache, war leader of the Mouache Ute under chief Tierra Blanca, rode at the head of the band of warriors. Sided by Eagle Wing, they rode silently, horses picking their way on the pine needle laden trail. They moved through the pines, narrow shafts of sunlight making mottled images dance across their figures, some covered with hair pipe bone breast plates others decorated with bear claw necklaces or beadwork fashioned by someone of their lodge. Some had a few feathers standing from a top knot of braided hair, others with long braids bouncing on their shoulders and chests. All wore fringed and beaded leggings, beaded breechcloths, and moccasins.

James Foley had bellied down below the widespread spruce branches, unmoving as he observed the passersby. Reuben crawled to his side, startling the man, for Reuben could move as silent as a hawk on the wind, even though he was moving on the bed of matted aspen leaves and pine needles. Foley frowned at the younger man but turned his attention back to the Natives. "Ute!

The leader is Kaniache. Ran into him before, he can be a mean 'un!" spoke the whiskery man in a soft whisper.

The cavalcade of warriors was stretched out in the black timber, some riding by twos, most alone. All carried weapons, from war lances to rifles, and held them at the ready. Foley added, "No paint, but could still be a raidin' party. Don't see no meat, so don't reckon they be huntin' neither."

The timbered trail was about fifty yards farther up the slope and in the thicker timber. As the warriors moved through the trees, Reuben lifted his binoculars for a closer look as he watched carefully and lay low beneath the long spruce branches. He turned slightly toward Foley, but the old man was gone! The prickly sensation at the back of his neck was the only warning, but he had learned to trust his senses and rolled to his side, bringing his Henry forward as he did and the arrow whispered past, cutting his buckskin jacket, his side and burying itself in the soil beside him. He swung the Henry between his knees and jacked a round into the chamber, dropping the hammer as the brass blade of the front sight aligned with the sweaty chest of the warrior, frantically nocking another arrow. The Henry bucked, the smoke blossomed, and the bronze chest sprouted red as the bullet split the solar plexus, stunning the warrior as his grip on his bow loosened and he fumbled with the arrow. Reuben levered another round, pulled the trigger, and added another red blossom on the warrior's chest, driving the man to his back.

The sudden blast of a rifle beside him revealed Foley on the other side of the tree, firing at his own target, another young warrior not ten feet from the first. An arrow trembled in the grey bark, showing he too had been a target. A glance to the second target showed the prone figure with the top of his head a bloody trench, as Foley growled, "Let's hightail it!" as he scrambled from his perch.

Reuben twisted around, searching the trees with wide eyes, surprised at the way Foley had slipped from his side so silently and without any word. With another glance toward the Indians now stopped and moving about, Reuben crabbed back from the tree and rose to a low crouch, turned, and trotted back to their camp hot on the heels of the whiskery old man.

They snatched at the reins of their mounts, hurriedly tightened the girths, and swung aboard. Foley led the way, laying low on the bony bay's neck. "C'mon!" he shouted without looking back for Reuben. The big blue roan twisted through the trees never more than a long pace behind the wily mountain bred bay. Branches slapped at them, doing their best to unseat the inter-lopers to the mountains, but both men glued themselves to their mounts, legs clamped tight and rumps growing roots in the hard leather seats.

The clatter of hooves on the rocky trail was inter-spersed with the sodden thumps of pine needle and matted leaves covering the thicker timbered path. Daylight showed ahead and Foley nudged his gelding to stay in the edge of the trees, picking his own trail. Reuben twisted around to look behind them, but nothing showed, yet he heard the muted screams of Ute war cries and knew they were in the run for their lives. He remembered there were at least a dozen and more warriors in the bunch, and having killed two of their number, even the hunting party would quickly become a vengeance-seeking war party, and they knew this country far better than either he or Foley.

Every long stride of the roan, the pounding of

hooves, the bobbing of his mount's head, the flaring of his mane, the smell of lather, the creak of leather, combined to drive the thoughts of Reuben's mind, calculating, considering, and formulating. He lifted up, looking ahead and slapped legs to the roan to drive him beside Foley. Reuben shouted, "We need to find an ambush, try to discourage 'em!"

Foley grinned, nodded, "Got it!" and nudged his mount forward. They were charging through the thinning timber, the trees growing sparse, when Foley crested a shoulder and just as quickly dropped below the crest. Reuben followed close behind, proud of Blue who had yet to falter in his steps or stride, even at the greater elevation and thin air of this mountain country. He had heard some of the miners talking and knew they were roughly around nine thousand feet above sea level, mighty high country for a lowland bred horse. Foley slowed, took a steep slope toward the bottom of a deep ravine, making them lay back over the cantle of the saddles as the horses slowly picked their way down the clay soiled hillside. Once at the bottom, Foley nudged the bay toward the lower end, then angled across the side slope to climb out.

Reuben's only thought was of the Ute warriors gaining on them, knowing they were leaving a trail a blind squaw could follow, but still he pushed on, encouraging Blue with a stroke on his lathered neck and soft words spoken. They crested the ridge and Foley motioned to a rocky shoulder that boasted lichen-covered boulders and scraggly cedar. Reuben nodded and grabbed his Sharps, slipping it from the scabbard as he swung his leg over Blue's rump and dropped to the ground. He tossed the roan's reins to Foley and scampered up the rocks, glancing to the trail behind them. He dropped behind a long flat-topped slab of lichen- and moss-covered limestone to stretch out the Sharps and settle into a solid shooting position. Foley had tethered the horses in a cluster of junipers and slipped beside Reuben.

With a glance at the old man, Reuben snatched his fur cap from his head and lay it on the rocks to rest his Sharps. Foley frowned, tempted to reach for his head cover, but let it lay as Reuben hissed and nodded to the far side of the big ravine where movement could be seen at the edge of the trees. The tree line was about six or seven hundred yards away and they couldn't make out the figures until Reuben lifted the telescope sight and focused. He whispered, "'Bout six hundred yards, they're hangin' back in the trees. The leader's motionin', prob'ly gonna send out some scouts."

"I know that war chief. That's Kaniache an' he's a mean 'un."

"Should I try for him, or one of the others?" asked Reuben, carefully watching through his scope.

"You can hit 'em from here?" asked Foley, incredulously, as he frowned at Reuben.

"How 'bout I scare 'em a little?" suggested Reuben as he narrowed his sight. He knew he could easily make a kill shot but didn't believe it would be needed. The war leader was at an angle to Reuben, his war shield showing just below the high pommel of the leather saddle. It was common for the natives to have a pommel or saddle horn that stood a good foot or more above the withers of the horse, giving both stability and protection for the rider, but the pale leather that covered the pommel, also made it a good target. Reuben focused in on the flat-topped horn, drew in a deep breath and let a little out as he began squeezing the thin second trigger of the Sharps.

The big rifle roared and bucked, spitting smoke and lead, sending the half-inch round lead projectile across the yawning ravine to explode the pommel of the saddle that was just inches from the war chief's belly. The scream of the chief, cries and shouts of the warriors, and the panicked whinny of the horse as he reared up in shock created instant pandemonium. The warriors scattered, tree limbs slapped and were broken off, saplings trampled, and at least two horses bucked and reared, unseating their riders and took off through the trees. Reuben watched through his scope, mindlessly reaching for another round, and quickly reloading. He closed the breech, his thumb on the hammer, but did not bring it to a full cock.

Reuben grinned as he watched the action, Foley was cackling as he too enjoyed the ruckus. The chief had landed on his rump, breaking only his composure, and shattering his dignity. His eyes flared wide as he looked at his panicked warriors and started to rise but paused to look across the ravine. Reuben chuckled as he saw the angry glare of the rumpled chief whose two feathers, so straight and proud before, now hung to the side, much like his pride.

Foley cackled, "Is that the chief there in the openin'?"

"Yeah, an' he ain't happy!" laughed Reuben.

"Can ya skeer 'em some more?"

"Sure," replied Reuben. He saw the chief's war shield that had fallen from the shattered saddle and lay on the ground near the chief's feet on the downhill slope. Reuben sighted in on the shield, choosing the thunderbird design in the center, and dropped the hammer on the Sharps. The rifle roared and the warriors scrambled, but not before the shield bucked and scooted a little closer to the chief. Before anyone could move, Reuben dropped the breech, reloaded the Sharps, and drew another bead. The second round went into the shield less than two inches from the first and the war shield split in the middle, the two pieces separated by a foot because of the impact.

Reuben reloaded, and watched, waiting, and wondering. The warriors stayed behind cover, but even at this distance, their grousing and shouting could be heard. He glanced to a cackling Foley who sat grinning and shaking with laughter, and asked, "Think they'll leave?"

"Dunno. Don't figger they ever been in a fix like this! But if'n they're smart, they'll skedaddle! Reckon Kaniache can see them last two shots coulda just as easily been twixt his eyes, an' if'n he's thinkin' right, he won't wanna be a target. He likes livin' too much! But of course, you prob'ly made him mad, an' maybe he's a thinkin' you made him look bad to his men. But we'll just hafta wait 'n see," he chuckled, still shaking his head and laughing. "I ain't had this much fun in a long time!" he added, slapping his buckskin covered knee.

M cCannon and Doc Bell rode side by side, sharing their thoughts about the recent killings and the men they pursued. Doc looked at McCannon. "These two that were said to be hidin' out by Tarryall can't be the same ones that you were chasin', can they?"

"Prob'ly not. But we know the two we tracked outta the valley of the South Platte are the ones that have been doing the killing, especially after we found the body of their last victim. He was cut up just like the others!" replied McCannon.

"Then why are we goin' after the men from Tarryall?" asked the doctor.

"Didn't you say the miners thought they were the murderers?"

"Yeah, but we know they're not."

"But we don't know what they are guilty of that would make 'em hide out and run out. Must be something terrible to make 'em cut n' run like that, don'tcha think?"

"Maybe, but . . ." mumbled Doc Bell, glancing to McCannon.

"We prob'ly won't even run into 'em, but if we do, we'll just find out what they are guilty of and handle things accordingly," declared McCannon, nodding as he spoke, the firm set of his jaw brokering no argument.

Doc Bell nodded in return, arching his back and twisting side to side. "Ain't used to doin' this much ridin' in a day!" he declared, trying to find a soft spot in the hard seated saddle.

McCannon stood in his stirrups, turned to the men following and called out, "McComb! Gilbert! You men come here," he ordered as he turned and dropped into his seat. As the men came alongside, he looked at them and nodded upstream. "You two scout ahead, see if there's any sign of two men on the run. If you do, hurry back an' let us know, but don't try anything your own selves, hear me?"

McComb, the older of the two men, nodded, answering, "Got it!" and dug heels to his horse and took off at a canter, prompting Gilbert to scamper to catch up. The two men disappeared around a peninsula of trees that rode a ridge from the crest of the lower end of Red Hill. The trail the posse followed sided the tree line well above the meandering Trout Creek in the bottom of the wide valley. The ridge that paralleled Red Hill was sometimes called the backbone of South Park because of the many finger ridges that carried run off from the long high ridge, resembling the backbone and ribs of a skeleton. Each finger ridge boasted timber on the north facing slopes, but little more than buffalo grass on the south slopes, the colors accenting the terrain.

With the valley between the ridges no more than a mile and a half wide, anyone coming from the north and taking the trail nearer the creek, would easily be spotted by the remaining men of the posse, even though most were already growing bored with the uneventful riding and looking, until the two scouts came back at a run, waving at the column of man hunters. McComb slid his mount to a stop before McCannon and started talking before the dust settled.

"Cap'n! We spotted 'em! Two men, down by the creek. You could tell they was hidin' out. Had their horses tethered in the thicket, but they was by the cottonwoods, had their rifles pointed upstream like they was waitin' for somebody!"

"Didn't see us, though!" added an exasperated John Gilbert, slapping dust off his legs with his hat.

McCannon quickly shouted his orders, splitting the remaining men into three groups and sending one group of three to the far side of the creek, the second into the trees to circle farther around and upstream of the targeted duo. He reserved the primary and larger group of himself and three others, Doc Bell, Julius Sanger, Frank Miller, to approach under cover of the thick willows on the west side of the creek.

McCannon stood, waved to the others, and the three groups charged into the little clearing, yelling, and shouting like a band of Rebels, totally surprising and scaring the two supposed outlaws. At the shouted orders from McCannon, "Drop your rifles and raise your hands or we'll shoot you dead!" without a shot fired, the two men dropped their guns and turned to face the posse, hands raised and eyes wide.

McCannon stepped down, approached the two men with pistol in hand, and growled, "What were you two up to? Who'd you kill? Didja steal some gold from a claim?" his questions rattled off without a pause for the two to answer. "What're your names!" he demanded, waving the pistol before him. As he barked questions, the rest of the posse slipped from their horses, with one man taking them aside and picketing the bunch. McCannon barked again, "What're your names?"

"Uh, uh, I'm Baxter 'n'," nodding to his partner, "he's Snyder. What's this about? Whaddaya want us for?" whined the first man, his pot belly hanging over his britches which were missing the top button and strained at the galluses. His bulbous red nose shone through his whiskers and drooping forelocks, black eyes showing fear and his knees shaking as he pranced about like a man in need of an outhouse.

"We heard you was running from Tarryall like a couple thieves! What'd you steal?" growled McCannon, still waving his pistol and moving about, glaring at first one then the other of their captives.

"We ain't stole nuthin'!" whined Snyder. A skinny man with scraggly hair that looked like last week's noodles had been dumped on his head and only a few stuck. His nose was long enough to smell tomorrow's dinner, and his pointed chin was a weapon in itself. Pointed shoulders gave him the appearance of an underfed scarecrow, and high-water britches showed high topped shoes with no socks.

"Then why's the whole town sayin' you did?!" asked Doc Bell, glancing from one to the other.

"I dunno!?" shrugged Baxter, holding his legs together fearful of an accident.

McCannon lunged toward the portly figure, cocking the hammer on his pistol as he did, pointing the weapon at the man's face, yelling, "You did so!" he barked, scaring the man even farther and prompting the feared event to happen. A collective moan rose from the men behind McCannon. Some shaking their head, others grinning at the man's embarrassment, a couple turning away.

McCannon glared at both men, slowly lifted his head, and let a grin split his face. "Alright then, you don't wanna tell us what you did, we'll just hang you anyway!" He turned away from the two frightened men that looked to one another and at the posse, fear painting their faces as Baxter started whining, "Nooo, nooo! We didn't do nuthin'! Honest!" he pleaded. But his cry fell on deaf ears.

McCannon turned toward the men. "Sanger! Miller! Get a rope an' throw it o'er that branch!" pointing to a big branch on the cottonwood that stretched overhead about twelve feet high. He turned and spotted another on a nearby tree, looked at the men and barked, "Endleman! Woodward! Put a rope o'er that branch!" As the men hurried to get the ropes in place, McCannon turned back to the captives and growled, "Last chance! Tell us what'chu done!"

Both men shrugged, holding their hands to the side of their shoulders, and pleaded, "Nuthin'! We done nuthin'! Honest to God! Nuthin'!"

Snyder added, "'Sides, you can't hang us without a trial!"

McCannon leered at the man. "You're having your trial now! Don'tchu wanna say what you did?"

"We're innocent! We done nuthin' that deserves hangin'!" whined Baxter.

"Doc! Tie their hands behind 'em! Sanger! Woodward! Put a loop around their neck!" All the men of the posse were frozen in place for but a moment until McCannon hollered, "Do it! Now!" Doc looked at the others, nodded, and walked behind the two men, strips of leather binding in his hands. He grabbed both hands of Baxter, started wrapping them and spoke to the man, "Better say somethin', I ain't sure but what he means business!" and tied him tight. He stepped behind Snyder, tied his hands, and slapped him on the shoulder. "Better speak up!" and walked away to join the other men, now standing in a semi-circle, staring at the men.

"Both o' you," stated McCannon, motioning to the two men that had been dispatched for the ropes behind each man, "grab hold o' that rope and pull 'er tight!"

The men did as instructed, pulling the ropes taut, making the two would-be outlaws stand on tip toes. McCannon barked again, "Well? What'dja do?" as he glared at each one.

With nothing but whimpers coming from both men, McCannon ordered, "String 'em up! Now!" and pulled his pistol to fire it in the air, making every man jerk in shock. The four men pulled the ropes, hand over hand, lifting the two captives off the ground, the nooses tightening on their throats, making their heads twist to the side. Baxter started yelling but was quickly silenced by the tightening of the noose. Snyder was kicking and choking, the rope chafing his neck as his eyes bulged out and he fought for air. McCannon shouted, "I can't hear you!" and looked at the men on the lifting end, "Drop 'em!"

All four men readily loosed the ropes and dropped the hanging men to the ground in a heap, but McCannon shouted, "Pull the ropes tight, don't wanna 'em getting free! Might hafta hang 'em again!"

The posse members frowned, looking at one another and at McCannon who was ignoring the rest of the men as he stepped closer to the victims. "You gonna talk?" and jerked at the ropes, loosening them from the chafed and burned necks, letting the pair gasp for air as they choked and squirmed. McCannon stepped back, looked at the four men and motioned for them to pull the ropes taut again. The tightening ropes forced the two to fight to their feet, stumbling and staggering until the ropes were taut again. They stood staring at the captain, shaking their head. Baxter choked out the words, "Wait, I got sumpin'," and coughed.

McCannon motioned for the men to hold their place as he stepped closer to Baxter. The man looked up at McCannon and with a raspy voice said, "Only thing I done was break outta jail at Park County. Only there for bein' drunk."

McCannon shook his head, stepped back and looked at the four men, "String 'em up again boys!" and watched, cackling, as the two men kicked and struggled, trying to free themselves as they were slowly lifted off the ground. McCannon watched, shouted again, "I can't hear you!" and laughed. The two men's struggles lessened, and their faces were turning pale and blue before McCannon ordered, "Drop 'em!" and the four released the ropes, dropping the pair to the ground.

Doc Bell went to the two men, knelt beside them, and loosed the ropes, then pulled the nooses off both the men. He glared at McCannon, spoke softly, "No more!" and looked back to the men, removing their bonds.

McCannon looked from the captives and to his men to see the disapproval on every face, but nothing was said. He looked back at Doc. "Alright, help 'em up."

Doc did as bidden, helping the two men to their feet, but neither moved away, still fearful of the men before them. McCannon looked at Snyder, then to John Landin, one of the men who stood by the horses. "Get Snyder's horse an' gear." He looked back at Snyder, "Now, you leave this country, y'hear? I don't wanna hear of you being anywhere near South Park ever again! You understand?"

Snyder hung his head, his hands on his raw throat, his eyes squinted as he stared hatred at McCannon, but he nodded and grunted as he turned toward his horse. Landin helped him climb aboard, handed him the rein, and softly said, "Sorry, we didn't know what he was gonna do." Snyder shook his head, dug heels to his mount and trotted from the clearing, turned south, and disappeared past the willows. McCannon turned to Baxter, "Now, for you. I'm gonna have a couple men take you into Fairplay, leave you with the soldier boys and they can take you California Gulch for miner's court. Now, get on your horse and don't try anything or we'll put that noose back on you!"

It was a quiet posse that rode from the willows around Trout Creek. Landin and Nathrop were tasked with taking Baxter into Fairplay as the others headed south to eventually meet up with the rest of the posse. Doc no longer rode beside McCannon, nor did the others. He rode alone, grumbling and mumbling to himself, thinking as most tyrants do that he alone was right and justified in what had been done.

21 / GETAWAY

"**D**usk is comin' on and they ain't gone yet! I'm thinkin' they be plannin' on getttin' 'round us and gettin' their revenge! All that shootin' done is make 'em want blood an' to get that there cannon away from you," declared Foley, squirming around behind the scraggly cedar, and trying to look across the ravine to the Ute warriors.

"What do you suggest?" asked Reuben, using his scope for a better look. Although it was evident most of the raiding party was still together in the trees, he also knew there was no way of knowing, short of seeing them move, if all warriors were still there. He had been thinking that if he were the leader of that bunch, he would be wanting a way to get the one who had shamed him in front of his braves. That meant Kaniache would be working every possibility of outflanking, surrounding, or attacking them before light was gone, or wait until the shooter was hindered by darkness and do an all-out assault.

"Dunno. Don't hardly figger we can sneak out without them knowin' it, but if we lay here, they're

142

gonna figger some way to get to us," surmised Foley, his fidgety manner showing his growing restlessness and even fear.

Reuben had been thinking about their getaway and had taken time to look over the lower terrain with his binoculars. He plotted out their moves in his mind, considering all the possibilities and knowing they would have to be calculated in their moves, certain in their timing, and lucky on all counts. There were over a dozen angry Ute warriors, and every single one was determined to have fresh scalps hanging from their coup sticks before the day was over. Reuben looked at Foley. "We'll need to shake 'em off before we go to the meetin' place. We don't want to bring them down on the posse."

"I doubt if any of 'em's there yet, and if they are, that'd just be more guns in our favor," suggested Foley.

Reuben pointed with his chin. "You get the horses ready while I shake 'em up a bit."

"What'cha gonna do?" asked the curious whisker face.

"Just get 'em ready," instructed Reuben, lifting the butt of the Sharps to his shoulder. Foley nodded and grinned as he slid on his rump down the slight slope, trying to be as quiet as the loose dirt and shale would allow, and grabbed the reins of both mounts, pulled loose the slip knots, and swung aboard his bay. He stood in his stirrups to look down the slight draw, trying to judge the best escape route and was startled by the rattle of pistol fire.

Reuben slipped his Remington pistol from his holster, lay it beside the rifle and used the scope to pick a target. He did not expect to hit anything at this distance with the pistol, but he wanted to give the Ute something additional to think about. He aimed at the top of the trees, knowing it would be sheer luck for any slug to reach across the ravine, but he dropped the hammer. With two quick shots, another single shot, and a delayed shot, he holstered the pistol and took a quick bead with the Sharps. He sent two slugs into the trees, guessing where the warriors had gathered, and the shouted screams told of his success. He reloaded the Sharps as he dug heels into the loose dirt and made his way to the horses. Quickly slipping the rifle into the scabbard, he took time to replace the cylinder in his pistol with a fully loaded spare. Dropping the pistol back into his holster, the extra cylinder into the saddle bags, he swung aboard and reined Blue around to take the trail down the draw.

They moved quietly, knowing they were out of sight of the Utes, but it was always possible Kaniache had sent out scouts to watch for any movement or attempt to escape. The soft adobe soil made their movement quiet, and they carefully moved the branches of the junipers as they passed, knowing the whisper of needles on their coats was a giveaway. Once clear of the timber, Reuben, now in the lead, turned Blue to the east, skirting the timber that fell from the last timbered sentinel of the southern foothills of South Park. Some had called this tree covered knoll, Saddle Mountain, and Reuben had spotted an aspen-lined cut between the bigger mountain and the smaller foothill to its north. If they could make the dense thickets of aspen, they could possibly lose any pursuit, or at least provide enough cover they could mount either another ambush or at least some sort of defense.

Blue stretched out, now free from the confines of twisting timber-lined trails, he pointed his nose and let his mane fly, enjoying the freedom of open spaces to run all out. He took in great gulps of clear mountain air, his muscles rippling beneath Reuben's legs as the two became one, with Reuben lying low on the blue roan's neck. With a quick glance behind, Reuben saw the lean bay with the whiskery old man atop, taking each stride with certainty and a smooth gait that belied his rugged features. There was no sign of any Ute in pursuit, but they wanted to put as much distance between them as possible before darkness fell.

They approached the long thicket of aspen that covered the lower flank of the taller mountain and slowed to a walk to give the horses a breather. Foley came alongside after twisting around in his saddle to look at their backtrail. "Cain't see nobody follerin' but they could be along just anytime!" He looked at Reuben, saw the determined cut in his visage. "What'chu thinkin'?"

"If we can get around that knob yonder," began Reuben, pointing to the east end of the lower ridge, "that'd give us several options as to where to go and such. If they're closer'n I think, we'll have to pitch a quick ambush and try to make 'em think we joined up with some friends."

They had come about three miles since their last stand and the sun was at their back and stretching the shadows out before them, shadows that appeared like gruesome waifs pointing the way to an empty land that promised little more than a lop-sided battle. "When I looked at that from our last stand, it appeared like there were good rocks near the crest. And if we can line out our weapons, move from one to the other and keep up a hail of bullets, we might convince them we have greater odds in our favor."

Foley shook his head. "Well, one thang fer sure, we ain't got nuthin' to lose but our hair!"

They rounded the point and angled up the opposing

slope that was dimpled with rocks and piñons, cacti, and cedar with a few larger junipers. A cluster of junipers sat just over the crest, no more than twenty yards from the chosen rocky rim and Reuben nodded and reined up. He dropped to the ground, slipped the Sharps and the Henry from the scabbards, grabbed the saddle bags with the extra ammo and nodded to Foley to take the horses to the trees.

With his Sharps and Henry placed about eight feet apart and on two good promontories that would offer ample cover, Reuben found a third position for his primary site. He uncased the binoculars and searched the valley with the aspen groves and saw no movement except the quaky leaves fluttering in the evening breeze. Foley found himself a couple positions, lay his Spencer repeater rifle at the first and unholstered a pair of Walker Colts and lay them on the sandstone slab before him.

Reuben chuckled when he saw the Walkers and asked, "Goin' to war, are you?"

Foley cackled, "Yeppir! An' I'm loaded fer bear! These have fifty grains of powder behind those conical slugs, and I can raise a sure-fire ruckus with these two sisters, yessiree!"

"With all that firepower, I might as well take a seat back yonder and watch!" chuckled Reuben, shaking his head at his whiskery friend.

Foley laughed. "I ain't even gonna unlimber 'em less'n I hafto, and that'll only happen if you let any of 'em get close enough! After all that shootin' you done, you pro'ly blasted 'em into last week!" cackled the old man, showing his wide grin that revealed his almost toothless mouth.

Movement at the corner of his eye turned Reuben

back to scan the wide draw and saw the band of Ute hanging close to the aspen and carefully picking their way, leaning low to look at the tracks left by the two white men. They were still about a thousand yards away and were being careful not to expose themselves more than necessary, the thickets of aspen yielding little in the way of trails or room to move through.

Reuben moved to his Sharps and settled down behind the rock cluster, propping the rifle across the stone, using his possibles pouch to rest the fore stock. He sighted through the scope, chose a bigger trunk of the white barked aspen about seven hundred yards away that stood beside the leader, and fired. The Sharps bucked and spat smoke, but Reuben had chosen a point where buck brush rose beyond the slab and would disperse the smoke, hiding his position. He saw the slug strike and smash through the soft wood trunk, exiting in a shower of bark and splinters that made those behind jump and shout. The leader, Kaniache, pulled the rein taut on his skittish mount as it sidestepped away from the tree, and Reuben saw the warriors and leader shouting and scampering.

"I don't wanna have to kill any more of 'em, but if they keep comin' I reckon I'll have to," declared Reuben as he dropped another cartridge in the breech and closed the lever. He looked through the scope again, watching the movement of the warriors.

"Well, you either scared 'em, or you told 'em where we are. Either way, sumpin's gonna happen right soon, I reckon," observed Foley. "And here I was thinkin' about a pot o' coffee," he drawled, shaking his head. "Guess that ain't gonna happen!"

They rose up out of nowhere! Where there had been clumps of buffalo grass, random bushes of sage, thickets of rabbit brush, now each seemed to birth a Ute warrior. Arrows came like lances of lightning amidst a mountain cloudburst, bullets whizzed by or ricocheted off the rocks to whine into the fading light. The setting sun blazed behind the attackers, blinding Reuben and Foley, who fired at shadows. Reuben pulled his hat brim low, lifted the Sharps and knowing the scope was useless in the dim light, sighted through the open sights, putting the brass blade on the chest of the shadowy attacker and dropped the hammer. The big Sharps bucked and spat flame and smoke, the bullet striking the screaming warrior in the throat, silencing him as he did a backward somersault down the steep slope.

With another round fired from the Sharps, Reuben didn't sit still long enough to see the bullet strike its target but dropped the Sharps and scampered to the Henry. Bringing the lighter rifle to his shoulder, the buckhorn sight aligned with the front blade, and he fired. The bullet blossomed red on the solar plexus of a bare-chested warrior as Reuben jacked another shell and fired at the charging warrior beside the first. The attackers' only disadvantage was the steep slope with loose soil and shale, making footing difficult and the two defenders let a barrage of bullets be the welcoming committee for the golden shrouded rim rock. The setting sun was putting on a display of gold lances and orange clouds, a beauty that would cause most to pause and enjoy, but the present circumstances did not allow such extravagances.

Reuben glanced to his right to see the wily old man, a big Walker Colt in each hand, laying down a blanket of lead, smoke encircling his whiskery face and balding head. A cackle that reminded Reuben of a frantic turkey, emitted from his toothless grin and the little man seemed to strut in time to the discordant music of death.

Reuben rose from behind the big rock, Henry at his side and he began walking toward the attackers, shouting, and screaming his own version of the Battle Hymn of the Republic, as he levered shell after shell into the chamber and fired a steady stream of lead, each projectile finding a target and oftentimes taking more than one with a single slug.

The sight of the two crazy white men charging into the face of the warriors struck awe and fear into the usually undaunted warriors. But the dead and wounded that littered the hillside, the constant thunder of the weapons in the hands of the fearless men that charged, turned the remaining warriors on their heels and first one, then another, and finally the remaining few vaulted the sage, tumbled over the buffalo grass and tripped through the prickly pear, letting nothing deter them from an escape.

Reuben and Foley stopped, glanced at each other, and began reloading. Foley had two spare cylinders behind his belt and quickly changed them for the empty ones. He slung his Spencer from behind his back and dug through his pockets for cartridges to reload. Reuben jammed cartridge after cartridge into the Henry, keeping his eyes on the fleeing Ute and glancing to the unmoving bodies around him. He had yet to unlimber his Remington revolver but touched the butt to reassure himself it still sat waiting, snug in his holster.

Both men sucked a deep breath of air tinged with gunpowder and the stench of death and blood but were relieved they were still standing and could breathe. With a nod to each other, they turned back to the rocks to retrieve the other weapons and horses. Nothing else need be said as both men swung aboard their horses, rifles resting across the pommels, and pushed the mounts over the shoulder of the hill and pointed them into the fading light and toward the distant timber-covered knob where they were to rejoin the posse.

E lly had been fraught with worry, unaccustomed to sitting behind while Reuben went into the fray of a fight. From their first meeting, they had loved, ridden, and fought side by side against Indians, outlaws, and rebels, and she was uncomfortable sitting alone and waiting. The first night of Reuben's absence, she had attended Preacher Dyer's Bible meetings with Horace and Augusta Tabor and went shopping with Augusta the next morning. Although she ordered a new dress from the dressmaker, she made do with the one she packed, alternating with the split skirts and blouses for everyday wear, but she had little concern for women's fashion and shopping, preferring her time with Reuben and their travels and adventures.

Her reverie was interrupted by a knock on the door of her room in the Pacific Hotel, "Telegram for Eleanor Grundy!" announced a boy's voice from the hall. Elly stood and went to the door, opening it to see a young man with a cap in hand and holding the envelope before him. "Eleanor Grundy?" he asked, smiling a nervous smile.

"Yes, I'm Mrs. Grundy," answered Elly, smiling to put the young man at ease. He offered the envelope and to his surprise, she handed him a coin, which he glanced at and smiled broadly, "Thank you, ma'am! Will there be a reply?"

"Wait a moment and I'll see," she answered, opening the envelope to extract the gram.

Have conferred with Holladay and we are agreed your appointments are permanent and you are free to use as needed. Your confidential work has been beneficial and helpful. Looking forward to your continued success. John Evans, Governor, Colorado Territory

Elly grinned, shook her head and looked at the young man. "No, there will be no reply. Thank you!"

The young man nodded, grinning. "Thank you, ma'am!" and turned away to retreat down the hall and stairs. Elly stepped back into her room, folding the telegram, and putting it back in the envelope to place it in her saddle bags that lay on the shelf in the chifforobe. She sat on the edge of the bed and Bear put his paws beside her causing her to absently put her hand on his head. The pup was growing fast and was already the size of most full-grown dogs, but the size of his paws implied he would grow even larger. His deep fur made him resemble his namesake, but his manner resembled more of a furball housecat.

"Well, Bear, looks like it's you and me for a while. I don't know about you, but I'm tired of this room," she looked around as she rubbed behind his ears making him cock his head to the side to savor the favor, "so what say we go for a walk, maybe even a ride. Anything to get out of this town and away from all these people!" The dog dropped to all fours, and bounded around the room, excitedly going to the door and back to Elly for attention and encouragement.

"Alright, alright. Let me get on some riding duds and we'll go!" she conceded, just as anxious as the big pup for a change of scenery.

With the dog beside her, most gave way to the two as they walked on the boardwalk to make their way to the livery and the stable with her Appaloosa mare. She wore her buckskin fringed jacket over her split skirt, her Colt pocket pistol holstered and hidden at her left hip, her Flemish knife seated snugly in its sheath between her shoulder blades. She was confident in her abilities with all her weapons and had no reason to be concerned for her safety, although a lesser woman would never be seen alone on the streets of Buckskin, even in broad daylight.

"Afternoon, Rufus!" declared Elly as she entered the livery to see the liveryman busy at his task of feeding the animals.

"Afternoon, ma'am! Goin' ridin' are ye?" asked the man, pitchfork in hand. He was a middle-aged man with a special made shoe that sported a four-inch sole to make his left leg the same length as his right. If someone didn't notice the shoe, the man's ability to get around was not hindered by the malady. A cheerful man, most everyone respected Rufus and he managed to make a good living with his livery, the oldest in the town.

"Oh, thought I'd get a little fresh air away from all the hub-bub and crowds. Bear here," nodding to the pup, "wants to stretch his legs and so do I."

"Well, don't be goin' too far, you can never tell about some o' these men. Most of 'em have been too long away from respectable womenfolk."

"Oh, I'm not concerned. I have found the men of the

west are usually quite considerate of ladies, and although they may be lonely, the remembrance of a loved one, a mother or a wife or sister, usually keeps them on their best behavior. And if not, Bear there would be happy to give them a lesson on respect!" she chuckled as she tightened the girth on her saddle.

"But he's just a pup!" declared Rufus, leaning on the pitchfork, and watching Elly rig her mare.

"He's already shown himself to be very protective and most folks are afraid of him because he looks and sometimes acts like a bear!" She led the mare from the stall and into the big open door, paused and made a slight hop to put her foot in the stirrup to swing aboard. She reached down and stroked the neck of the Appaloosa. "Are you ready for a jaunt out of town, Daisy?" she asked, running her fingers through the mare's mane. The horse bobbed her head as if she understood and stepped out in response to Elly's leg pressure. She turned to see Bear run to catch up and stride alongside the spotted mare, glancing up at Elly and back at the horse, tail wagging as he bounded along, obviously happy to be on the run.

Curious about the gold prospecting and mining, Elly chose to go upstream to have a look at the different operations. With many of the smaller claims manned by one or two men, they used rocker boxes or sluice boxes, a few had the longer sluices with rerouted water from the higher streams, diverting the water through the long boxes with ripples in the bottom to catch the heavy gold, letting the watered-down soil pass through. A muted roar came from around the bend and Elly nudged Daisy toward the trail that rode the shoulder of the north hills and overlooked the valley. She reined up when she saw the hydraulic mining with its high-powered nozzles driving the pressurized water against the hillside, washing the soil into the long sluices and more.

A hodge-podge of log cabins, board huts, dug-outs, tents, and lean-tos, dotted the hillsides taking up any flat place untouched by the claims. Men were huddled around rocker boxes, sluice boxes and a few washing pans, all with dreams in their eyes and hope in their hearts. With only an occasional glance at passersby, a few recognized Elly for the woman she was and those few took a lingering look at the strange sight of a woman riding alone in gold country. One man mumbled to his partner, "If I had that waitin' fer me, I'd be a mite anxious to get through with the day's diggin's!"

"If you had that waitin' fer you, you wouldn't be here in the first place!" growled his partner.

"Mebbe we oughta do sumpin' to make sure that'd be waitin' fer us in our cabin ever' day!"

"What do you reckon you, ugly as you are, could do to get a fine-lookin' woman like that to be waitin' fer you?" grumbled the grungy man at the end of his shovel as he hefted another shovel full into the sluice box.

"She's gotta come back that same way, don't she?" cackled the first man as he sorted through the catchings of the sluice ripples. He stepped back from the sluice and shaded his eyes as he watched the lone riding woman round the point of the trail that went to the upper reaches of the wide ravine.

———

THEY RODE BY THE LIGHT OF THE MOON, TIRED BUT WARY, fearful of being pursued by the remnants of the Ute raiding party, but hopeful they were alone on the trail. Staying in the deep shadows of the tree line, they moved quietly, listening to the distant wail of a lonesome coyote, the scream of a circling osprey, and the rattle of crickets that hovered in the sage. Foley was in the lead, and he traveled a familiar trail. They had agreed it would be best to find the rendezvous point with the rest of the posse and make an early camp.

Reuben pushed the blue beside Foley's bay, and spoke lowly, "Doesn't seem like anybody's on our tail, but I'm gonna hang back in the trees, wait a bit and see. You say that camp we're bound for is on the north side of that hill yonder?"

"Ummhmm, it's set back in the trees a bit, but I'll be watchin' for you and call you in, long's you don't have anybody on your tailfeathers!"

Reuben nodded, pulled Blue to the side, and ducked into the nearby cluster of junipers. The dark trees would give good cover for both him and his horse, as well as a good view of their backtrail. He dropped to the ground, Henry in hand, and loosely tethered Blue to the nearest juniper. He had already picked a break in the trees for his observation point and dropped to one knee beside the bigger tree. A quick check of the backtrail, a glance to his rifle, and Reuben relaxed. His thoughts turned to his wife, safe back at the hotel in Buckskin, probably sitting in on Preacher Dyer's meetings and enjoying the company of Augusta Tabor. It was good for a woman to have the company of another woman on occasion. Reuben knew there was some special bond between women, even newly acquainted women. His mother had often told him and his brothers that although men had a camaraderie unique to their gender, women also had a bond that was special and never understood by men, but a bond that needed to be nurtured from time to time.

He grinned as he thought of his blue-eyed blonde,

pretty as a peach on the outside, but full of fire on the inside. He smiled at the memory of the times they fought side by side against both Indians and outlaws and knew she was a handful, and remembered the advice of both her father and Little Raven, the Arapaho chief, when both said she was going to be tougher to tame than a wildcat. He chuckled at the thought and brought his mind back to the present and searched their backtrail again.

A glance at the stars told him it was time to go to the rendezvous point and maybe have a bit of supper, perhaps some coffee, before turning in for the night. He was certain they were not followed and was relieved to think that the Ute had chosen to gather their dead and return to their village. But they would still take turns standing watch, for one can never be too cautious in Indian country.

F oley had built a small fire in a hole, shielding the light and flames with a couple of pieces of sandstone slabs stood on edge, and had the little coffee pot dancing at the edge when he used the cry of a nighthawk to summon Reuben into the little clearing within the thicket of junipers. He stood with his rifle cradled in his arm as he watched the long-legged blue roan quietly pick his way by the light of the moon to carry Reuben into the trees to the campsite. Reuben nodded, spoke quietly, "No sign of any followers. I'm hopin' Kaniache decided to pick his fight another day and another place. I'm tired of runnin' and hidin'." He slipped to the ground and quickly stripped the gear from Blue, letting him roll in the grass and dirt, then rubbed him down with handfuls of the thin-bladed Indian grass. Reuben glanced to Foley. "Coffee smells good!"

Foley nodded, returned to the fire, and used his neckerchief to lift the hot pot from the coals and pour them each a cup. He handed the steaming brew to Reuben, cocked his head to the side to give more of a critical look at his partner, then dropped his eyes to his cup, letting the steam circle his nose as he sipped on the thick java.

"You're almighty quiet! Somethin' botherin' you?" asked Reuben, enjoying the coffee as he sat on the log, elbows resting on his knees as he looked at Foley.

"Cain't figger you. You come from nowhere, join up with the posse and ride like you was a greenhorn to the country, but when it comes to facin' down them Utes, wal, I ain't never seen the like!" He shook his head, took another sip, "You ain't from 'round'chere, and you ain't got no claim or nuthin', so why'd you join up wit' the posse, anyhoo?"

Reuben sipped his coffee, his glazed eyes showing he was considering his response, then looked up at Foley. "Why'd you?"

Foley pulled his head back like a startled snapping turtle and snorted, "Humph! Reckon cuz this here's my country! I got a bit of claim up in the hills, don't tend it much, and I built me a cabin, so, I guess you could say it's muh home! An' anytime some outlaw comes along an' threatens that home, e'en if I ain't got a woman an' kids an' such, then I'll do what I can to make things right! Ain't that what a man's s'posed to do?"

Reuben grinned, chuckled, "Reckon." He looked around, avoiding looking at the dwindling flames and checking the dark shadows of the trees, "And I've got a wife, back there at the Pacific Hotel, but I don't have a cabin or a home, but I want the country to be safe for my wife. But it's more than that. I heard about what a posse did to a couple men they thought needin' hangin' and without a trial, they did just that. When I heard about this posse, I saw the same look in some of the men's eyes and I thought maybe I should tag along to do what I could to keep that from happenin' again."

Foley frowned, looked from Reuben to his coffee and back again. "I was gonna ask what you, one man, could do to stop a posse of a dozen or so men from hangin' another outlaw, but I seen you fight, so maybe you could stop it. But you're still just one man . . ." he let the thought hang in the air between them.

Reuben nodded, unconsciously touched the pocket of his jacket where the deputy's badge lay, and looked at Foley again. "Well, sometimes when a man has right on his side, there might be other things that weigh in his favor."

Foley frowned, looking at his friend, for Reuben's movement to his pocket did not go unnoticed and Foley wondered, just what those 'other things' might be and what secrets were still carried by his friend. It was not uncommon for men of the west to harbor many secrets; some fleeing a past that haunted them, some carrying burdens that weighed heavy upon them, some with lives that were extreme opposites of what they chose to live here in this new land where a man could make his life anew and forget a shadowy past, and many chose to do just that.

"Somebody's comin'," hissed Foley, moving away from the firepit and into the trees. The shuffle of horses' hooves through the soft soil and deep grasses told of two horses approaching, slowly but steadily. A voice called out, "Hello the camp!" and the movement of horses stopped.

Foley answered, "What's yore bizness?"

"We're friendly! Part of a posse from Buckskin! Can we come in?"

"Come ahead on but keep yo' hands high!" crowed Foley, staying in the trees.

As the two men came into the clearing, the blue light

of the moon showed familiar figures and Foley stepped from the trees, "Wal, if it ain't Bill Youngh and Joe Lamb! Step on down, fellers! We done drunk all our coffee, but if'n you got the makin's, there's the pot!" he nodded toward the small fire.

The two men grinned as they swung down and began stripping the gear from their horses. Once they finished, they picketed them near the others and returned to the fire. Foley looked at the pair, who appeared to be a mite tired and asked, "Fellas see anythin'?"

Youngh nodded as he sat down, letting his partner tend to the coffee making, "We found a trail that might be them, o'er towards the headwaters of Oil Creek, but can't be sure."

"See any Injuns?"

Youngh frowned, shook his head. "Nary a one! You?"

"Oh, no more'n a couple dozen. Ol' Kaniache an' his boys sorta disinvited us from the country, but Reuben convinced them we done had us an invitation to this here party!"

Youngh frowned, looking from Foley to his partner, Lamb, and then to Reuben. With another glance to Foley, he looked at Reuben. "Don't rightly reckon I know you." He stretched out his arm and hand, "I'm Bill Youngh and that there's," nodding to his partner by the fire, "Joe Lamb." Reuben took the offered hand of Youngh, nodded to Lamb, and sat back with his refilled cup and sat quiet, letting Foley do all the talking.

"They still around?" asked Youngh, glancing from Foley to Reuben.

"Nah, don't think so, reckon they tucked tail and left," drawled Foley, doing his best to keep a straight face. He looked up at Youngh, "See any the other fellas?"

"Nope. But I reckon they'll be comin' in come daylight."

Reuben caught Foley's eye as he tossed the dregs of his coffee, and spoke just loud enough for him to hear, "I'll take first watch. I'll wake you in 'bout three, four hours."

Foley nodded and watched as Reuben slipped into the darkness.

Youngh looked at Foley. "There's somethin' you ain't tellin'."

"Mebbe. I'll wait till the others get here so I don't have to repeat myself," drawled the mischievous old man, grinning as he went to his blankets. He added over his shoulder, "I'm takin' second watch an' I'll wake you for your turn!"

Lamb looked at his partner, "Didn't think we'd need to have a watch."

"They said they run into Kaniache and his Utes, so, might be wise," answered Youngh.

REUBEN SAT ON THE BALD KNOB AT THE EAST END OF Three Mile Mountain, a rock escarpment his bench and the wide panorama of South Park before him and the snake like South Platte River with its beaver ponds and willow groves below him. The slow rising sun was off his right shoulder and was just threatening to show its face to add color to the eastern sky when the rippling stream tossed silver coins of light from its cascades, lighting the way for early morning game to get their daily drink. He had spent his time with the Lord, praising Him for his bounty and protection, asking coverage for his wife and the men of the posse, and finished his time thanking Him for the new day. He stood, stretched, and slipped the binoculars from the case and scanned the wide terrain for any sign of life.

Two riders showed themselves on the far side of the river, following a dim game trail from the Puma Hills that framed the east edge of South Park. Reuben guessed them to be the other scouts, Spaulding, and Carter. He turned to the north and west, looking for any sign of the rest of the posse, supposing it to be too early to get a bunch like that on the move, and the only life he spotted was a small herd of Pronghorn, a couple of stray buffalo, and what appeared to be a small bunch of wild horses. With another quick but fruitless scan, he stashed the field glasses away, tucked his Henry under his arm and started back down through the trees to return to camp.

Foley had the coffee going, some johnny cakes sizzling in the pork belly fat in the frying pan, and a plate with the strips of bacon that drew his attention. Foley grinned at his partner, "Did'ja see anythin'?"

"Looks like the other scouts are comin'," nodding toward the river bottom, "but that," pointing to the bacon and johnny cakes, "will be long gone 'fore they get here!"

It was several hours after Spaulding and Carter came into camp and the sun was high in the afternoon sky that Captain McCannon and the rest of the posse came into sight and soon joined the others. All were anxious to get out of the saddle and get something to eat, and Reuben had fetched some fresh meat when he bagged a young buck going to the river for his morning drink. The long strips of backstrap sizzled over the fire and were soon snatched up by the hungry men that had been long on the trail.

163

McCannon called the three groups of scouts together to get a report and looked to Spaulding and Carter first. "So, you fellas cut any fresh trail on the east side of the Park?"

Carter was the first to respond, "No, Cap'n, only thing we saw were a few greenhorns tryin' to find where all the gold was hidin', and of course several Pronghorn, buffalo an' mule deer."

"No Mex looking types?" asked the Captain.

"No, Cap'n, nary a one!"

McCannon looked to Bill Youngh and Joe Lamb. "Billy, you and Joe were s'posed to cover the lower end of the Pumas, the road going over Wilkerson Pass, and that stretch of open park on the south end. Find anything?"

"Well, Cap'n," began Bill, "we did cut several trails, but most had more'n two riders. We followed up a couple, but they were gobackers, you know, them greenhorns that quit diggin' and decided to go back where they come from," he chuckled at the memory of the times he considered giving up himself, but looked to the captain and continued, "but late yestiddy, we cut a trail that looks promisin'. It was . . ." but he was interrupted by a ruckus among the other men. The captain looked at the others, suspecting it was just a tussle over the choice strips of meat, until a spinechilling scream came from one of the men that brought everyone to their feet.

"NO! NO! NO! DON'T HANG ME! HELLLP ME MAMA!" the man known as John Endleman was thrashing about, appearing to fight an invisible foe, screaming, and crying, and started to run from the camp, but another man tackled him and straddled him, putting his hand over his mouth, trying to quiet the man. Doc

Bell joined the others as they gathered around the two, each offering advice but none with a solid solution.

Julius Sanger had straddled Endleman and now jammed a neckerchief into the man's mouth while two others held his arms down. Doc Bell spoke softly to the man, "John, John, it's me, Doc Bell! Settle down, John, there's no one tryin' to get to you!"

Wide eyes stared up at the Doc as Endleman thrashed about, shaking his head side to side and trying to kick the man off his chest. Sanger glanced to the Doc. "Whatta we do, Doc?"

"He'll tire out soon, just hold him down, so he doesn't hurt himself or anyone else!"

It was a good while later that Endleman seemed to run out of energy or fight and seemed to relax. Sanger leaned back, still holding both arms, and looked at his friend. "You alright now, John?"

The prone figure did not answer, nor did he thrash around anymore. Captain McCannon came close and summoned two other men to help and instructed, "Get him up, and if you think it's safe, then let him free, but if not, you might have to bind and gag him. We can't have him bringing every Injun in the country down on us!"

The three men did their best to keep Endleman under control, giving him coffee and food but staying within reach of the man. He ate and drank, but was nervous and jittery, always looking at the three men beside him as if he was waiting for a chance to escape, but they stayed near until the captain told them to keep him bound and gagged and tethered through the night, and if he was alright come morning, then they would do something else, but offered no firm solution to the dilemma.

No one slept sound that night, several volunteered to

stand watch knowing the only peaceful place was away from the camp. It promised to be a long night, and the captain had to plan their pursuit of the killers as well as tend to the man that had lost his mind, a true test of his leadership.

Enjoying the ride into the mountains, Elly scanned the high rising granite tipped peaks that seemed to be reaching up to scratch the bellies of the few clouds lazily drifting across the vast blue sky. She noticed the narrow-bottomed draw between the high mountains showed a contrasting green to the empty ruggedness of the rocky mountains whose shoulders bore only rough grey and brown talus slopes that held a narrow fringe of deep green timber. But it was the timber that was getting sacrificed in the rush for gold. Where there had been thick stands of ponderosa, fir and spruce trees, wide bald spots with the pox of low stumps now scarred the big shoulders of the mountains.

She reined up, sat with arms crossed on the pommel of her saddle, and scanned the countryside, now marred with lean-tos, dugouts, and sod-covered log cabins. But the scars nearer the water were deeper and trashier, with the remnants of broken dreams scattered like the remains of a tornado. She shook her head and nudged Daisy off the trail to cross Buckskin creek and start her return to the hotel.

Because of the lay of the land and the headstrong snow-fed stream, there were more claims on the southwest side of the creek. More activity among the miners did not keep them from noticing the passing of a pretty woman. Most stood, stretched, and waved with a lustful grin on their faces, but no one gave Elly the idea she might not be safe. Men of the west were known to have high regard for women and treated them as they should be treated. But there were always those few that thought themselves above or exempt from any law and would always choose to go their own way regardless of the supposed restrictions of the law. Yet this was a lawless land, with most things handled by a miner's court or as had already been demonstrated, by the quick action of a posse.

As Daisy picked her way on the narrow trail, Elly watched all about, enjoying the birds, flowers, and the friendly greetings of the men, but she didn't come on this ride to see men, she had wanted a quiet place of solitude with the trees and the scenery before her, not the ruins of gold-hungry miners. The trail bent through the scattered trees to crest a low finger ridge and reveal a cabin set back against the steep slope and having several tall trees round about. As Daisy picked her way down the steep trail, the gravelly bottom making good footing rare, she came to a short stretch that rode the shoulder and offered a view of the canyon. She paused and took a moment to enjoy the view, but her reverie was interrupted by a gravelly voice, "Well now, what do we have here?" The man who spoke stepped from the trees and grabbed the reins of Daisy up close to the bit to hold her head and control her.

"Let go of my horse!!" demanded Elly, pulling back on

the reins, and tussling with the long ends, thinking of using those long ends as a whip against the man.

Another voice answered as he stepped from the trees, "Looks like a woman to me! A mighty fine-lookin' woman, too!"

The first man was built like a whiskey barrel, his broad beam having busted the two lower buttons on his linsey Woolsey shirt showing a big bulge of thick black hair. His shirt was unbuttoned and showed a similar sight at the throat where the chin whiskers blended with the hair on his chest. Tobacco stained and rotted teeth showed as the slash of a mouth that cackled, making his belly jump. Black eyes peered from under the thick fur of eyebrows, and matted long black hair showed itself too thick for even a curry comb. His moniker was Black Mike, and he snarled at Elly, looked at his partner, Nikko, and said, "Yup, just like I figgered. She's purty, got some meat on her bones, and she'll make us nice an' cozy come wintertime, won'tchu honey!?"

"Let go my horse or I'll call the law down on you!" threatened Elly, showing nothing but anger in her flashing blue eyes. She glanced around for Bear, but he was nowhere to be seen.

"Hah! You hear that, Nikko? She's gonna call the law down on us!" he cackled again, letting his belly dance as his shirt fought to keep it contained.

The tall skinny man with a hooked nose that seemed to be best friends with his pointed chin, let his eyes flare as he drooled, looking at Elly. He snickered, "Honey, ain't no law here in these mountains! We can do whatever we want and ain't no lawman comin' after us!"

Elly leaned forward, crossing her arms on the pommel, and glared at the big man holding Daisy's reins. "There's always Sam's law!" she growled, glancing from one man to the other. A movement of black behind the men caught Elly's eye as she saw Bear step quietly to the edge of an escarpment that forced a bend to the trail. He was close enough, that if she gave him any sign, he could pounce on the shoulders of either man.

Black Mike frowned, glanced at his partner. "Sam's law? You ever heard of Sam's law?"

"No, Mike, can't say as I have." He shook his head and looked at Elly and asked, "Just what is this Sam's law?"

"Samuel Colt," she said, a grin splitting her face as she held her Colt pocket pistol before her, pointing it at Black Mike, but watching Nikko as she motioned him closer to Mike. "Now like I said, let go of the reins!" She cocked the pistol as she spoke, never wavering nor showing any fear, letting Big Mike stare into the one-eyed monster held in her hand. "NOW!" she demanded, nudging Daisy forward, pushing against the dirty stinking miner that thought himself to be a one-man roadblock. But Daisy shouldered him aside, making him stumble and back step to catch his balance. A deep throated growl got both men's attention as they looked behind and above them to see the big black wolf/dog snarling and showing his teeth. They looked from the dog to the woman and Elly could see the big man was calculating a way out of his predicament.

Elly reined Daisy up and turned to face the two men, moving the pistol back and forth to keep the men away. "Now, I'm going on down to town, and I better not see the two of you anywhere in town, because I will tell everyone what the two of you tried to do, and if you show your faces, they'll prob'ly get up a lynch party real quick! And I'll provide the rope!"

"You ain't gonna shoot! That thing ain't big enough to do no harm! Now, why don'tchu put it down and come on into our cabin," offered Black Mike, sidestepping away from the rocks without looking at the dog and holding his arms out to his side.

"Yeah! An' we got gold! We'll pay you!" suggested Nikko, getting a stern frown from his partner.

"I don't want your gold and it'd take more gold than these mountains have," waving her pistol about to indicate all the mountains, "just to get me off this horse! Now, back up there against that boulder . . ." she was interrupted by Black Mike who quickly bent down and drew a big knife from a boot scabbard and was cocking his arm to throw it, but the bullet from Elly's pistol drove into the man's elbow, shattering bone and splitting an artery. Blood started spurting as the big man dropped to his rump, holding his arm. Bear lunged from the rocks to land before Nikko, head down as he assumed a stance for an attack, growling and snarling at the skinny man as if sizing him up for dinner. The blood was running through Black Mike's fingers, and he was growling and whining, "Get me a doc or sumpin'!" he demanded, looking at his partner.

"I'll go to town, try to get a doctor or something!" She looked at Nikko, "Try to get him into your cabin and wrap that arm in bandages of some sort, or he'll bleed to death!" She motioned to Bear and dug heels to the Appy and disappeared into the trees, bound for Buckskin to search for a doctor. But she knew real doctors were rare in these mountain towns, yet most towns had some semblance of a doctor, be it a horse doctor, a blood-letting barber, or a mid-wife, while oft times there would be a skilled professional healer with a shady background that had come west for the same reasons so many others left their homes and families: the riches of gold.

Elly entered the town at a gallop, coming to a sliding

171

stop in front of the Pacific Hotel where a couple old-timers and their old dog sat watching the doin's in town as they rocked in their cane-style chairs.

Elly looked at the men and asked excitedly, "Is there a doctor in town?"

The old men shook their heads, one removing a pipe and asking, "What's the hurry, ma'am?"

"There's a man that's been gunshot, he's bleeding bad and needs a doctor."

"Then you go to the livery, ask for Doc Wiggins, he's the closest thing to a doctor we got!"

Elly nodded, grabbed up the reins of Daisy, swung aboard, and with Bear at her heels, headed to the livery at a canter. She heard the chimes of hammer and anvil before she was near the door, and smiling as she slid to the ground, she asked the smithy, "Doc Wiggins around?"

Without missing a lick, the smithy nodded to the first stall where Elly saw two stocking feet protrude from under the gate. She went to the stall, saw an unkempt man snoring as he lay in a big pile of dry husks, half covered. She kicked his foot, bringing him instantly awake and sitting up, "Wha . . .What'chu kickin' me fer?"

"You Doc Wiggins?"

"Yeah, so?"

"So there's a miner that got shot an' he's bleeding real bad. He needs your help!" declared Elly, trying to prompt the man to action.

Wiggins rubbed his eyes, yawned and stretched, then called out to the smithy, "Hey, Smithy! Can I borrow a horse? Got a patient that needs me!"

"Go ahead, take that sorrel in the stall next to you! There's a rig on the fence."

He frowned at Elly. "How's come you know about this man?"

"He is Black Mike, and his partner is Nikko. They got a claim and a cabin just this side of the big bend, south side of the creek."

"I know who you mean. I can find him. But you didn't answer my question, How's come you know them?"

She dropped her eyes and answered quiet like, "They tried to kidnap me, take me to their cabin."

"Then seems to me you'd want him to bleed to death. And yet you came and got help, hmmm." He paused a moment, tightened the girth on the saddle then turned to face Elly, "Who shot him?"

"I did. And I'd do it again!"

The doc, still a little bleary eyed, looked at Elly. "I bet you would, too!" and chuckled as he mounted up. He pointed to the black bag that sat on a storage bench, and Elly grabbed it and handed it to the doc, who smiled and chuckled, shaking his head as he nudged the sorrel into the street.

"**T**his is good," declared Felipe Espinosa as they rode into the black timber to find a wide clearing with dusty shafts of sunlight illuminating the glen.

"But there's no water?" whined Vivián, knowing he would have to hike wherever and fetch water for them both.

"There's water below the cliff, there's plenty grass there also. We'll picket the horses, hobble 'em, and they can get water whenever they want." He held a satisfied smirk on his face, mischief or evil showing in his eyes. "Anybody finds 'em, we can pick 'em off from up here!" He tossed the reins of his mount to his younger brother and nodded. It was enough of an explanation for Vivián, what Felipe meant was for him to strip the gear from both horses, lead them back down the trail, rub them down and picket them for the water. He would also be expected to carry the bags and canteens of water back to camp for coffee.

With a curt nod, Vivián led the horses to the uphill side of the clearing, choosing the shade of a tall ponderosa, and began stripping the horses. It was just a short while later that he led the horses to the secondary clearing, picketing and hobbling them well apart but within reach of water. He stood, stretching, and looked around. His brother had chosen a good site, the cliff face appeared as if the Creator just stacked several layers of rock to make a sheer wall behind the horses. With a dead snag protruding from a slight shelf and scattered buck brush hanging from any crevice that allowed, the bald face of the cliff showed the strength of stubborn seeds planted by random birds or tumbling pinecones. At the base of the cliff, chokecherry bushes were in abundance and willows were scattered along the dry creek bed that would only see ample water if a good cloudburst were to wet down the dusty foothills, but a bubbling spring filled a small basin, big enough for the horses and packing water.

Vivián thought his brother had chosen wisely, as usual, and arguing with him did no good but often stirred up his quick-to-blow temper. He bent and twisted to peer through the trees at the trail they followed, and it was difficult to see which also meant it would be difficult to be seen. Vivián dropped his eyes and started back to camp, idly kicking at the tall grasses and random rocks.

He began to remember, to relive, those days in the San Luis Valley when the soldiers from Fort Garland came into their village and killed and raped many of the people. That was the event that finally stirred Felipe and his brother Vivián, on the road to revolution. After picking up the bodies of his wife and daughter, carrying them to the shed to make rough caskets, the two brothers had committed themselves to revolution, and the taking of lives in vengeance for what had been done to their families.

As he pushed through the trees, it was like he was pushing his way back to his wife, Mary, and his daughter, Angelina. He was startled when he stepped into the clearing to see Felipe with a small fire going, awaiting the return of full water bags. Vivián handed one off and took the others to be stacked with the gear. As he returned to the fire, he asked, "How long will we stay here?"

"Our horses need a good rest, so do we, and I don't think anyone is following us. So, I thought we would spend a day or two here, away from everything and everyone, so we can plan what we will do." Vivián nodded in understanding, relieved for the break and time to rest.

———

"Reuben, you and Foley there, since you've already had a get acquainted meeting with Kaniache and his warriors, how's about you two taking point and see if you can find the trail Billy Youngh told us about."

Reuben nodded, turned away and sided Foley as the old man said, "Looks like we be together again! Suits me. You?"

"Sure, that way I don't have to get used to another greenhorn!"

"Greenhorn! You're the onliest greenhorn around'chere!" blustered Foley, slapping Reuben on his back. "By the way, what's this 'extra power' you talkin' about?"

"Extra power?" asked Reuben, confused at his expression.

"Th'other day we was ridin' and you tol' me why you joined the posse, and when I asked what one man could do, you said somethin' about havin' some 'extra power.'"

Reuben nodded, remembering the conversation, and added, "I think I said somethin' about when a man has right on his side, he usually wins."

"Yeah, that was what I was talkin' 'bout. So?"

Reuben chuckled, dropped his eyes to the trail. "Well havin' right on your side gives you more confidence and motivation to stand up for what is right. In this case, it's not just about catchin' some killers, it's also about what a mob can and will do when they are far away from civilization and there's no established law in the land."

"Hmmmm, I think I know what you mean. Did you hear what the posse did 'fore they come down chere?"

"No, what happened?"

"Well, they caught those two that the doc tol' 'em about, and McCannon kinda went looney, had this hate in his eyes, and he made the men hang them two!"

"Again!?" asked Reuben, reining up to look at his partner.

"Yup! Hung 'em 'twict'! Let 'em down both times, wanted to hang 'em agin, but the men wanted no part of it. So, he had some fellas take one that confessed to some thievery, into Fairplay. He let the other'n go cuz he had nothin' on him. Warned him to get out of the territory!"

Reuben shook his head, looking down at the loose dirt on the trail and mumbled, "Well, at least they didn't kill anybody."

AFTER REUBEN AND FOLEY LEFT THE POSSE CAMP, McCannon gathered all the men together to give his orders for the day. He summoned Billy Youngh and Joe Lamb. "You two, I want you to go to where you found those tracks and follow 'em. If you get too close, back off and come find us, and if you run into Foley and the other'n, join up with 'em. We'll be moving slowly in the bottom of the valley, following Oil Creek." He summoned Thomas Wells, nodded, and said, "Tom, I want you to take half the men, and take Endleman into Canon City. There just ain't no way we'll ever get close to the killers with him shouting and yelling!"

"Does it make any difference who I take?" asked Wells.

"No, no. But this is Ute country, although I don't think you'll be in any danger, and I want you to have enough men to defend yourselves, but on the other hand, if you kinda picked out any you think might not make the grade if we come to a shooting party, then that would be wise and appreciated."

Wells grinned, nodded, and turned away to select his companions for the ride to Cañon City. If they made good time, they might make it all the way to Cañon before dark. That would be a warm bed, hot food, and maybe even a bath. He just wasn't used to spending so much time in the saddle, and they weren't done yet.

The rest of the men, eight in all, begrudgingly swung into their saddles, moved a bit to find a soft spot for the sores already forming, and sighed heavily as they looked into the maw of the canyon that held Oil Creek, and perhaps the two killers that had set everyone's nerves on edge. They hoped to finish the chase today but were prepared to take a few more days if absolutely necessary.

John McCannon rode side by side with Charles Carter, the owner of one of the largest trading posts in the gold fields, offering every item and tool a prospector would need, and able to order in big machinery whenever some lucky miner hit it big and wanted more.

Carter was of average size, curly hair in a Monk's cut with the shiny top of his head showing red from the unrelenting sun. They rode quietly, settling into the easy gait of the horses and using the quiet time to observe their surroundings.

They came from the timber on the north side of Three Mile Mountain and were now south bound beside the little trickling Oil Creek. To their left rose a long timber covered ridge that held many Ponderosa, Spruce, and Fir. But lower and closer in, the terrain was populated with bunch grass, Rabbit brush that was beginning to show bright yellow buds, sage, gramma, buffalo grass, and many different cacti, with prickly pear and cholla being the most proficient. The only bright green was that growing near the creek in the valley bottom, but it also carried different flower beds, lilies, Indian paint brush, blue Larkspur, and several pretenders to the daisy family like the Black-eyed Susan, Mountain Gumweed, and others.

Reuben and Foley had already covered this ground and were on the trail of the killers. Billy Youngh and his partner had returned with a negative report and now rode behind McCannon and was summoned forward to look at the tracks. "That the trail you were following?

Youngh stepped off his horse and went to one knee to look at the tracks closely. He stretched out his hand and lightly touched the tracks, his eyes moving from one to the other and with a nod of his head he rose and looked to the captain. "Yessir, that looks like the same pair. The bigger horse had a notch in his shoe and that's the same."

"Good, good. Can you tell how old those are?"

Youngh dropped to look at the tracks again, comparing the nearby tracks of the killers to the tracks of Reuben and Foley, then looked up at the captain. "Reckon these were made early yestiday, maybe even a little earlier."

The captain nodded, glanced to Youngh. "Come along then, we've got to make up some time!"

R euben and Foley rode silently, the sun high in the cloudless blue sky. They had been on the trail for just over half a day, working out the tracks of those they thought to be made by the two Mexican killers. They had ridden around a steep gorge that Foley knew and had said, "There ain't no trail for man or beast through that there gorge. We can take a roundabout way off to the right yonder, through that thicket of trees."

It was a steep sided, rocky gorge that made the small creek roar like a big river, but it was a short stretch and within about a half mile, they picked up the tracks again, siding the creek. A little less than three miles farther, the creek joined a larger one and Foley said, "That there's the one they call Oil Creek. It wanders through them hills yonder, and it's kinda like an old man in his rockin' chair, once he gets to talkin' he can go on and on and take forever to get anywhere! That's what that durned creek is like, it wanders all over and takes forever to get anywhere!"

They sat side by side looking at the green of the valley bottom, made so by the meandering creek.

B.N. RUNDELL

Although willows, alders, chokecherry, and service berry bushes crowded the creek, often obscuring it from view, the moisture fed the grassy flats that covered the valley bottom. Foley pointed to their right and downstream, "Over yonder's a saddle notch," he pointed and looked at Reuben, "see what I mean?"

"Yeah, 'pears to cut through the trees and ride that shoulder a mite 'fore it crosses over."

"That's it! That's the trail. Now, lookin' at these tracks, I think these two just followed the crick, an' if'n we take that trail," nodding toward the notch, "we might make up a little time on 'em."

"Suits me! Lead the way," directed Reuben. They sat loose in the saddles as their mounts drunk deep of the cool stream. Foley pulled his mount's head up, reined him around and pointed him toward the trail in the trees. Reuben followed close behind. "We gonna find a good place for noonin'?" asked Reuben, talking to Foley's back.

The old man cackled, "Oh you betcha! This ol' man ain't goin' too far 3

'fore we stop for coffee an' such!"

And he was true to his word. After riding a little less than five miles across the rolling plains of the massive mesa, they took to a dog-leg ridge that held juniper, cedar, and piñon on the northeast face. It wasn't a trail that Foley followed as much as a sense of direction. He had been through this country a few times before and as was the way of the traveling men of the time, he catalogued and memorized every tidbit of knowledge he had of the area; some from other men that had explored or prospected the country, and from his own travels.

In the lead, Foley came to the point of the ridge and started to swing his horse around to take to the dim game trail that traversed the rimrock on the west edge of the ridge, but movement below caught his eye and he quickly slipped to the ground, dropped the reins to ground tie his mount and hunkered down to go to the point of the long ridge. Reuben mimicked his moves and followed the man, rifle in hand and binoculars hanging from his neck.

They dropped to their bellies and scooted closer to the rim. Foley whispered as he pointed, "I think it might be Kaniache and his bunch." Although they were over five hundred yards below them and a forest of trees and bushes separated them, Foley thought it necessary to whisper. Foley rested on his elbows and watched Reuben use the binoculars to locate the source of movement. What he saw was a band of Utes and they appeared to be readying for a hunt or an attack on something. It was a camp on a grassy flat at the convergence of High Creek and Oil Creek. He counted at least fifteen warriors, all busy with their weapons. He also counted weapons and as near as he could tell, four had rifles of some sort. If they were the usual trade fusils, they would be flintlock and not very accurate. Because most warriors could fire off six or seven arrows in the time it took to reload the rifle, they preferred the familiar weapon. But the status given to one with a white man's weapon prompted many to seek after them.

"I don't see any paint on any of 'em," explained Reuben, handing the binoculars to Foley for him to take a good look-see.

"And as near as I can tell, they got more horses than warriors. That could mean they either had a raid and stole 'em, or they're gonna use 'em to haul the game back to their village."

He scanned the scene below, nodded, and handed the

binoculars back to Reuben. "Trouble is, that's where I figgered on havin' our noonin'!"

Reuben had lifted the glasses for another look and as Foley spoke, he replied, "Well, I know for certain if those Ute knew how cantankerous you get when you don't get your coffee, they'd hightail it outta there real quick like!"

"I'm about to get cantankerous with my ridin' partner if'n he don't figger out where we can get our coffee."

Reuben rolled to his back, shading his eyes from the glaring sun, and said, "Looks like they're 'bout to move on anyway. Maybe that blackbird tol' 'em you were gettin' upset!"

Foley snatched at the field glasses and took another look. "Sure 'nuff! Wal, that means we can go 'head on and start down there. By the time we get there, they'll be gone, and the shade'll be just right for a short snooze!" While he spoke, he was crabbing back from the point. He stood to a crouch, looked at the edge to be sure he was not in a line of sight of those below, and started to the horses. Reuben followed and both men swung aboard their mounts and started to the trees.

They broke into the open when the trail bent back upon itself and pointed to the south again, showing a dry gulch that carried the old trail. The east shoulder of the deep gulch was freckled with juniper and piñon, and the steeper west ridge was thick with the same trees. The trail they followed hadn't been used by anyone other than deer or maybe antelope and desert bighorn sheep. "I'm thinkin' we'll pick up the killers' trail after we get to the bottom," proclaimed Foley.

Reuben thought about it a moment and asked, "Wouldn't their trail alarm the Indians?"

"Uh, yeah, I reckon. But we don't know fer sure if'n they took the same trail."

As they neared the edge of the trees, Foley turned back in his saddle and gave Reuben the silent signal, dropped off his mount and in a crouch, made his way to the broad juniper that stood at the edge of the trees above the little creek. He dropped to one knee, looking around then stood and walked down to the creek and bent down again. It was evident he was examining tracks and he stood and returned to the trees. He spoke softly to Reuben, "They went upstream of High Creek, prob'ly takin' an old trail that goes into the buttes west of that wide flat we just crossed."

He stepped aboard his bay and nudged him forward and led the way to the same clearing where the Ute had been, moments before. Foley dropped to the ground and began looking at the sign left by the Ute warriors to get an idea of what they were planning. He moved around bent over, mumbling to himself, pointing, dropping to the ground to look more closely. He looked up at Reuben, "I'm thinkin' this ain't no huntin' party." He held up a flint shard. "See here," pointing to the tip. "This here's a point for penetratin', it's narrow all the way, but it broke on 'em so they started over. A huntin' point is broader, to cut through the hide but also to shed more blood and weaken the animal so they can catch up to it. But for war, they just want the arrow in the body, cuz that'll stop most people."

"Where do you think they're headed?" asked Reuben, stepping down to join Foley.

"No tellin' with them Utes. Could be headin' to raid another village, they do that sometimes, you know, against the Cheyenne, the Apache, even the Comanch!"

"Or they could be going after white men or a settlement," stated Reuben.

"Ummmhmmm, but I think it's Kaniache and his

185

bunch. But you know, the way they were actin' was like the village ain't too fer away," mused Foley, standing and looking around for any indication of a village. He paused, shaded his eyes, and pointed to the southeast. "There, smoke, ain't much and it's hard to tell, but that could be where the village is, and that's where Oil Creek widens out."

Reuben looked around, then went to his horse and withdrew the field glasses from the saddle bags, slipped the Henry back in its scabbard and withdrew the Sharps. The telescope was still mounted on the Sharps and Reuben checked his pockets for more cartridges for the Sharps. Satisfied, he said, "I'm goin' up there," nodding to the timber covered ridge that dropped into the valley of Oil Creek. "There's a high point up there, prob'ly take me a half-hour to get there, but it'll give me a good view of the area. Maybe I can spot the village, but I'm also lookin' for those two Mex!"

"While you do that, I'm gonna get us some coffee goin'!"

R euben could see the lodges of the Ute camp, counting about thirty lodges with busy families carrying on the usual duties that come with the closing of the day. Children, never concerned about time, were playing a hoop game while others mimicked the usual activities of their fathers and worked at fashioning bows and arrows. The women were bustling about as they were preparing for the evening meal, but several would be without their men who were part of the raiding or hunting party already seen by Reuben. Some of the women were working on stretched hides, scraping the last of the fat, flesh, and membrane. As near as Reuben could determine, most of the hides were of deer and elk, but one appeared to be the bigger bison. There were several men that had gathered at one of the lodges and were sitting around the fire, talking, and gesticulating at one another. He spotted one ancient looking man that sat alone before his lodge and appeared to be working on a long-stemmed pipe, carefully fashioning the bowl.

Reuben lowered the glasses and leaned back against the dead snag of the cedar tree, pondering the way of the

Indians. He had learned a lot since he left the army, having met, and dealt with the Pawnee, Cheyenne, and others, and he knew it was hard for many white men to picture the natives as families doing much the same thing that white families did at times like this, just being families. Most white people had never met a native or talked to one, and of course, very few had been in a native village to see the similarities with white villagers. Too many had formed their opinions and judgments based on what others said or some flamboyant newspaper reporter had written. Something they would never do about other whites in villages different from their own.

Reuben shook his head and dropped into a seated position, using his knees to stabilize his elbows as he lifted the field glasses for another look. He searched the far side of the creek, looking for a giveaway that would tell about the Mexican killers they were after. He slowly moved the binoculars upstream from the village, focusing on the far side or the eastern bank. He let a slow grin cross his face as he whispered, "Gotcha!" He was looking at a narrow trail that sided the creek just beyond and above the thick willows and it was evident it had been traveled recently, but only by a few horses. He had already noted the trail on the west bank of the little creek the Ute took to and from their camp that crossed over the little finger of land that pushed the creek into a wide bend around the point. He scanned the area again, mapping it in his memory, and slowly rose to return to the camp below.

Foley had been true to his word and had a little cook-fire going, dug into a bit of a trench, and lying just below the outstretched branches of a white-barked aspen. The thin tendril of smoke fought its way up into the branches, but the quaking leaves dispersed it and waved away any sign of a fire. Reuben grinned at the whiskery old man, appreciating his skill to focus on the need of the present instead of the potential, good or bad, of the future. "See anythin'?" asked the almost toothless pioneer.

"Yup. There's a whole village of Ute just around that bend, maybe thirty lodges or so, and that bunch we saw ain't the half of the number of warriors in that village." He stepped toward the fire, glanced at Blue as he grazed beside Foley's bay, both content with the grass and close at hand water. "I think those two fellas we're followin' crossed over the creek and took to a trail the other side of the water. But that village would have forced 'em to find another path but the only way we'll find it is to go over there and track 'em down."

"Could you see it ver' far?" asked Foley, frowning at his friend.

"Little ways, but that trail rides the slope of the east bank and unless any of the Ute went that way, they'd not see it. However, once around the bend, the creek kinda hugs the west hills, and leaves a nice wide flat for the village on the east side. That's why I said they had to take to the hills or somethin', because that trail leads right into the camp."

Foley shook his head, lifted the coffee to his lips and noisily slurped up a mouthful. He nodded to Reuben to pour himself a cup while he leaned back against the grey log beside the fire. He glanced up at the sun, guessed there to be maybe four hours of daylight left and looked at Reuben. "We got enough light to foller it out, see where they went, but we'll for sure be needin' to watch our backs and such; them Ute are a crafty lot."

"You reckon we have time to give the horses a good rest and get a little food for ourselves?"

"Sure, sure. But as far as food's concerned, I reckon we'll hafta settle for some smoked meat or anythin' else you got along with you."

Reuben chuckled. "I got a hand full of three-day old biscuits if that suits you?"

"Only three days? Why that's plumb fresh! Drag 'em on out here, my friend."

THEY CROSSED THE CREEK TO TAKE TO THE TRAIL THAT sided the stream but kept near the willows. The trail rounded the sharp bend and from their place beside the willows, they saw the bend that pointed the stream to the east. Reuben was in the lead and stood in his stirrups to see the prominent trail that left the arroyo bottom to climb over the peninsula of land that blocked the view of the upper reaches of Oil Creek. It was obvious this was the trail commonly used by the Ute, but Reuben's survey was interrupted by Foley, "Here's the tracks o' them killers!"

Reuben twisted around to see Foley on one knee, examining the tracks as he pointed to the small finger ridge that came from the long line of timber covered buttes to the northeast. "They prob'ly seen that village and decided to go 'round it. I reckon we should oughta foller 'em," suggested Foley.

"How far back you reckon the captain is with the posse?" asked Reuben, looking at their backtrail.

"Half a day at least!"

"Hope they don't run into that Ute war party or whatever it is."

"Ahhh, there's 'nuff fellers in that bunch to keep an

eye out. But you'n me need to foller this trail and get away from that village yonder. If we come on them Mex 'fore the captain gets here, we might have ourselves a bunch o' trouble."

"Then let's get a move on while we still have daylight. I don't hanker to come on those two after dark!"

The trail of the killers cut back on itself as they climbed the razor back ridge, then dropped over the east side and into a long gully that pointed them back to Oil Creek. Foley took the lead and broke from the timber to scout out the longer valley that held the creek. They were below the village of the Ute, and the tracks of the killers sided the little stream. Foley dropped to examine the tracks, guessed them to be a little over a day old and moving at a canter. He stood to look upstream of the trail and could see the smoke of the village. With another glance to the sun to calculate the daylight hours, he motioned to Reuben to join him and swung aboard his bay gelding. As Reuben came alongside, "If we're gonna foller them Mex, we need to shake a leg outta here 'fore some o' them Ute sees us!"

"You're leadin'!" declared Reuben.

They stayed near the tree line, wary of any Ute that might be returning from a hunt or a raid. After a couple miles, the creek meandered at the base of a talus slope that marked the beginning of a long gulch sided on the west by a steep-sided mesa marked by rimrock that hung over the edge, looking like a legion of demons staring down at any passersby that dared enter their domain.

They rode silently, the soft soil muffling any sound of footfalls and the tracks of the killers showing as nothing more than slightly disturbed dry soil. To look closely at the tracks revealed little, but to look at the line of tracks before them, showed the pair to be moving fast even

191

across this shoulder that held little vegetation other than cacti. But the soft soil gave way to rocks and sandstone, making footing a challenge and the tracks before them dropped off the shoulder to follow the creek and ride the grassy banks.

Several times they went into the shallow water when the east slope dropped suddenly into the creek, the rocky slope offering nothing in the way of footing for a trail. The rimrock hung about five hundred feet high over the arroyo bottom while the steep west slope with random cedar and piñon clung to rocks and ridges to adorn the slope with freckled greenery. It was slow going for a little more than two miles when the creek seemed to push back the rugged foothills, forcing them to give way to the persistent flow of the determined waterway. Instead of a long line of rim rock hanging high above, yet a narrow gulch split the same rim rock that appeared to slowly descend into the arroyo, making the west side nothing more than a wide talus that intermingled with sheer cliffs of granite, limestone, and feldspar. But light was fading, and Foley chose a grassy flat beside the creek just below that narrow gulch that split the rimrock to make their camp for the night. As Reuben came alongside, he explained, "Don't wanna run onto them Mex in the dark. Figger we oughta make camp 'fore we go any farther, what say?"

"I agree with you. I noticed the tracks of those two showed they slowed down, prob'ly lookin' for a campsite themselves. 'Pears to me they took to that gulch yonder," nodding his head to the split in the rimrock on the west edge of the canyon. Reuben looked at the sky and the surrounding terrain. "If you don't mind, I think I'll climb that ridge there, take a last looksee while there's still a little light."

"Go 'head on, I'll fetch us some firewood an' maybe get a fire goin' for some coffee. You shinny on up that hill an' I'll take care of the horses!" declared the old timer, grinning at his energetic partner. "Better you than me. Don't reckon I could climb back in my saddle, much less get up that slope there," nodding to the steep slope behind them, that Reuben had chosen for his reconnoiter.

It was just a short while when Foley looked up from his coffee to see Reuben bounding and sliding down the slope toward the camp. Foley dropped his coffee, snatched up his rifle and looked around for any others that might be chasing after Reuben. But the broad grin on Reuben's face did not belie any danger. Foley shook his head, "Now I know I make good coffee, but . . ." Before he could finish Reuben interrupted, "I think I spotted their camp. The creek takes a turn to the south, while across the flat up there," pointing to the cut in the rimrock, "there's a gulch that comes in from the northwest. I saw what looks like their tracks goin' into that gulch and I'm pretty sure I got a glimpse of the glow of a cookfire." He paused, chuckled, and looked at Foley, grinning. "They're prob'ly just like you and can't do without their coffee!"

"How far ya' reckon?"

"Less'n a mile!"

"We'll need to put our heads together with the cap'n in the mornin', can't let 'em get away this time!"

After a restless night, Reuben rolled from his blankets and slipped on his moccasins. He nudged Foley with his toe and spoke softly, "C'mon ol' man. Time's a wastin'!"

Without moving or opening his eyes, Foley responded, "Oh hush, young'n. I'm sayin' muh prayers!"

Reuben chuckled. "That's what I'm gonna do, but we need to palaver first!"

The full moon hung in the western sky, shining so bright it cast a pale blue blanket across the land, adding an air of mystique to the beginnings of the day. But Reuben thought every day was a mystery to be solved, not by laying around or idly wasting time, but by searching out answers to the unwritten and unvoiced questions that always accompanied the unknown.

Foley crawled from his blankets, stood in his holey socks and stretched and yawned.

"These nights just ain't long 'nuff no more!" He sat on the log where his boots waited, shook them out to rid them of any night creatures that had taken refuge, then tugged them on, tightened the laces and stood to stomp his feet into the time worn foot holsters. He looked at Reuben. "So, what'cha gonna do?"

Reuben went to one knee, grabbed up a stick and began to draw in the dirt. "We're here. Now the creek there takes a sharp bend to the south as it comes outta this canyon, but they took to that narrow defile that split the rimrock and crossed the flat to take to a gulch that feeds from the northwest. There's a bit of what looks to be a spring fed creek that flows into this creek," pointing to the creek beside their camp. "Now it appears that their camp is back up in that gulch with the little creek. On the east side is a long ridge, and another one just like it on the west side, but that one has rimrock, just like this'n. The bottom of the gulch is thick with willows and such, and the west ridge has an overhang of rimrock. Throughout that gulch, there's big rocks, escarpments, and such. I reckon their camp is pretty well protected, based on what we seen of their previous camps.

"Now, I'm gonna take my time, work my way up the east ridge that prob'ly overlooks their camp. If I can't see into their camp, I'll climb higher on the hill behind it until I can get a view of where they might be layin' about."

Foley looked at the crude dirt map, nodded, then looked up at Reuben. "What'chu think the cap'n oughta do?"

Reuben grinned. "I don't think he'll listen to any ideas from either of us, but if you can, you might encourage him to send somebody up the gulch beyond the west ridge to get above their camp, then he could come up from the creek straight into the gulch. I can cover 'em from up high."

Foley chuckled. "You got the cap'n right! He don't like to listen to nobody! But I'll try to explain it to the young pup!" He paused, looking around. "Ya reckon I can fix some coffee?"

"I don't see why not. Our camp can't be seen from where they are, unless one of 'em climbs the ridge, but I doubt they'll be doin' that." Reuben grinned at his friend, "But I'm gonna shanks mare it outta here so I can be in position 'fore the sun gets up."

THE SUN WAS BENDING ITS RAYS ACROSS THE TREETOPS and searching out the shadows of the many ravines, gulches, and arroyos when Captain McCannon and the remaining riders of the posse were hailed by Foley. The captain nodded to Foley, came near the man and leaned on the pommel and looked at the wiry old timer. "You found 'em?"

"Wal, I didn't, but my partner sho'nuff did! Step on down an' I'll show you on his dirt map where they be!"

The captain motioned to the men to dismount and water their horses as he followed Foley into their makeshift camp where the horses were tethered, and the coffee pot rested beside the hot coals. The captain looked from the pot to Foley and nodded with eyebrows raised, and Foley said, "Go 'head on! Don't think there's much more'n a cup left, but if'n you want, I can brew some more!"

"One cup'll be enough. Now, the map?"

Foley motioned to the scratching in the dirt and the captain came close, glanced back to the others, and looked at the map. Foley began and explained the scratchings the same way Reuben had described them and said, "Now, I ain't no cap'n, mind you, but it seems to me we'd be smart to send 'bout ha'f the men up one side and get above 'em, and the rest could come up from the creek an' we'd have 'em boxed in! 'Course, I think you'd prob'ly already figgered that out, didn'tcha, Cap'n?"

"Where's your partner?" asked the captain, looking around the camp.

"Oh, he headed out 'fore first light. Said he was gonna take the high ground and see if he could get a better look at their camp. He said he'd be up on this ridge," pointing to the eastern ridge beside the camp of the killers, "and could cover ya'll from there."

The captain huffed, shaking his head. "Ducking out on a fight is he?"

"Oh no, Cap'n. He's got him a Sharps and I've seen him shoot the feathers off an Injun from four or five hunnert yards!"

"Malarky! Ain't nobody can do that! He musta been aiming at something else and had a lucky strike!"

Foley just grinned, slowly shaking his head, and waited for the captain to re-examine the map and make up his mind about what they would do to try to take the murderers. Foley sat down on the log, nursing the last of his coffee and only casually looked sidelong at the captain. Within a few moments, the Captain stood, tossed out the dregs of the coffee and dropped the cup beside the stack of gear, and strode to the waiting men beside the horses.

"Alright, men, we're getting close. Foley tells me his partner is scoping out the camp of the murderers and keeping a watch on them. We'll tether our horses here and split into two groups. Younagh, I want you to lead one group and I'll lead the other." He paused, looking from one man to the other and began singling them out. "Sherwood, you and Fredricks will go with Younagh and Foley. The rest of you men will come with me. Now the

197

way Foley tells it, the camp of the murderers is up a gulch that runs into the creek here. There's a ridge on either side and, Billy, you and your men will take the west ridge, keeping it between you and their camp, Foley'll be with you and keep you going right.

"Now, Carter, Sanger, Lamb, you'll be with me, and we'll move into the gulch from below. We'll need to move quietly and keeping to the cover. We'll take our time to give the other group enough time to get in position." He paused, looking from man to man, then asked, "Any questions?"

"Are we sure these are the right ones?" asked Fredricks.

"I'm pretty sure they are, but since we haven't seen them yet, we'll need to take it slow and be sure. But don't get yourself in a bad spot trying to get a look at them. You just might get your head shot off!"

The men shuffled around a mite at that remark, yet each one knew what they were doing was dangerous and what the captain said could happen easy enough. None of the men were experienced man hunters, but they knew it had to be done. If these were the killers, they had to be stopped for the sake of everyone in the territory, for these men had murdered more than anyone knew and would not stop unless they were caught and dealt with and dealt with severely.

"Alright now, ready your horses, make sure you have enough ammunition. Billy, your bunch has to swing wide of the flat up top, pick your way across and around until you get enough cover, then move to the trees. But you'll need to leave your horses at the edge of the trees and move in on foot. Now, let's get started 'fore those two skip out on us."

The captain led the posse from the camp, climbing

through the trees on the narrow trail into the cut. He was staying close to the buck brush until they topped out of the cut, then picked his way from one cluster of junipers to another, always watching the mouth of the gulch where the murderers were suspected to be hiding. They stayed on the east edge of the flats, taking advantage of the terrain and spotty cover, until they came near the two ridges described by Reuben. The captain held up his hand, dropped to the ground and motioned Foley alongside. "That look like the ridges and the gully Reuben described?"

"It do shore 'nuff!" replied Foley. "He said there was a switchback of the creek at the mouth of the gully, just like that there," nodding his head toward the mouth of the arroyo. They were peeking through the piñon at the end of the long finger ridges that ran from the northern hills into the flats and pointed into the valley that carried Oil Creek.

"Then you go with Youngh, swing wide of these flats and come up on the far side. Looks like there's enough tree cover to make it into the draw on the far side. We won't start up the arroyo until we see you go into the trees. We'll hold back to give you a little extra time. We'll watch the gulch, make sure they don't escape out thisaway."

Foley nodded, looked to Billy Youngh, and motioned for them to move out. Sherwood and Fredricks, both prospectors that had seen a little success at their diggings, followed somewhat sheepishly, both wondering why they volunteered for this posse when they could be working their claims and making money.

· · ·

REUBEN HAD EASILY MADE IT TO HIS CHOSEN PROMONTORY before the sun showed its face in the east. The long ridge that sided the willow strewn gulch had rimrock that overhung the narrow draw, and the top edge had a smattering of gnarled cedar and twisted piñon. He found a pair that seemed to be competing for the little patch of soil between the lichen-covered rocks, and dropped to one knee for his first survey of the narrow valley below. It was too dark to see much, so he took the time for his usual morning prayer vigil and sought the face of the Lord.

Although still in the darkness and deep shadows of early morning, the bright light from the slow setting moon offered enough of the pale blue illumination for Reuben to give the valley a scan. He slowly moved his gaze along the willows in the bottom and searched out any offshoot draws that might hold a campsite. He made sure his figure was cloaked within the deeper shadows of the nearby trees and slowly moved only his eyes. He scanned the valley bottom, then scanned from the upper reaches back along the slope of the far ridge and into any narrow defiles that were masked by the dim light.

It was the glow of a campfire that gave them away. While most outdoorsmen are careful with their fires, keeping them shielded with rocks or nearby trees, these had either forgotten about the glow that shows in the early morning, or they had grown too confident and unconcerned. Reuben marked the location by the overhanging rimrock and the nearby talus slope but frowned when he could not make out the form of any horses.

He waited, watching, unmoving, as the slow rising sun began to give its light to help Reuben in his search. Then he saw them, two horses, hobbled on a little patch of grass below the camp and the overhang that offered shelter and cover to the men. But the necessity of water and graze for the animals, gave the men little choice but to picket them where they were, yet Reuben was certain the men would move the horses to better cover, come daylight. He sat back against the big rock that split the two trees and waited for some sign of the approach of the posse.

R euben had a clear line of sight to the tethered horses and part of the outlaw camp beneath the overhang. He was hopeful of seeing something that would definitively mark these two as the murderers they thought them to be for he wanted no part of a lynch party that would string up the men who may be innocent prospectors or passersby.

While he waited, he mounted the scope on his Sharps, tightened it down and lifted it to his shoulder to ensure it was in line and properly positioned. He aimed at the horses, saw one lift his head and look back toward the camp as it nickered to greet one of the men that was pushing his way through the trees toward the horses. At the same time, the other horse lifted his head in alarm, ears pointed and head bobbing slightly as he looked to the trail beside the creek. Reuben swung his scoped Sharps down the cut, saw movement and recognized the captain stealthily moving through the thickets near the little creek and knew there would be others.

It was difficult for one man to move through brush and thickets quietly, nearly impossible for several untrained man hunters to move silently. The horse that watched, looked from the brush to the trees and back again. The first horse, a black stallion with the only color being his left front leg showing a white sock, nervously pranced about, lifting his hobbled front feet as he moved closer to the second horse, a blood sorrel with a blaze face and three stocking feet.

Reuben drew up his knees to rest his elbows and steady his Sharps. Sighting with the scope, the early morning light at his back, he saw slow movement in the trees between the camp and the grassy flat where the horses were tethered. He held his rifle steady and moved his head to look at the approaching men of the posse, spotted a line of rocks that bordered the brush and hoped the captain would stop there. They moved closer, and the movement stopped as they came to the rocks and dropped on their knees to use the boulders as cover. They had spotted the horses and were waiting.

Reuben was hopeful the captain had followed his suggestion and sent some of the men up the back side of the west ridge to come down on the camp of the outlaws from high ground. He moved his scope along the brush and counted three men besides the captain. He moved his scope back to the horses just as one of the outlaws stepped into the open. Reuben let out a breath when he saw the man arrayed in the typical attire of the Mexican gaucho, tight pants over boots with big rowel spurs, short matching jacket, and sombrero.

Now Reuben was certain these were the men that had killed so many and disfigured and mutilated their victims. Reuben followed the man with his scope. The trees were thick with many dead snags and scattered boulders giving cover to the outlaw, but Reuben kept his scope focused on the man's movements as he silently eared back the hammer of his Sharps and rested his trigger finger alongside the trigger guard. He would wait for the captain to make the first move.

The captain had dropped behind the big rocks at the edge of the arroyo, motioned the others to take cover as well. He knew it would take a while for Billy Youngh and the others to get in place, but he had spotted the movement through the trees and recognized it was the horses of the murderers. But there was no camp, just the horses and he knew they would have to be patient, both for the movement of the outlaws and for the rest of the posse to get into position. He breathed deep as he scanned the terrain searching for the camp but realized with the tree cover as thick as it was, and the scattered oak brush, cacti, and dead snags, they could be anywhere. He looked back at the horses, saw one of the animals staring his way and knew they had been spotted by the horses, but still saw nothing of the outlaws, until there was movement that showed one man entering the little grass bench with the horses.

The captain motioned to Joe Lamb to come beside him, and the man crawled slowly, keeping the rocks between him and the horses. "You think you can hit him?" whispered the captain. Lamb nodded and slowly rose to his knees, and positioned his long Springfield rifle, using the flat rock shelf as a rest for his elbow. He watched the outlaw go to one knee beside the sorrel horse and begin to remove the hobbles. Lamb narrowed his sight, took a deep breath, let out a little and squeezed the trigger. The big .58 caliber rifle bucked and roared, sending the Minié ball to its target.

The bullet struck Vivián Espinosa in the side, dropping him to the ground, but the outlaw crawled to a rock, drawing his pistol as he moved and peered between the rocks to spot his attackers. He squinted, grabbing at his side where he was hit and brought his hand before him to see the blood. It was dark red and Vivián knew he had been hit in the lung, but he could still draw breath even though it hurt worse than being kicked by a mule, an experience he remembered from his youth.

Joseph Lamb was pleased with his shot, but carelessly stood, with only a scraggly cedar between him and the outlaw, to reload the long Springfield. He bit off the end of the paper cartridge and poured the powder into the muzzle and readied the Minié ball just as the captain growled, "Get down, you fool!" Lamb realized what he had done and immediately dropped to the ground behind the rocks.

Vivián looked through the trees to the rocks at the edge of the creek and lifted his pistol to take aim. He saw the hat of one man moving behind a low rock and squeezed off a shot. He dropped back behind the rock, struggling to breathe, every move excruciating, and wondered if Felipe would come to his rescue. He glanced to the trees where the narrow trail came from the camp and saw nothing.

He rolled back to his belly, moving side to side to see the shooter or shooters beyond the rocks and aimed at the edge of a flat sided rock, knowing the bullet would ricochet and possibly hit someone, maybe give him a chance to try to make it to the trail back to their camp. *Madre de Dios!* He whispered to himself, knowing his wound would probably be the death of him. He struggled to his knees, readying himself to stand and run to the trail. He rose and lifted his pistol, just as a shot came from the attackers, but his sorrel had spooked and jumped between Vivián and the rocks, taking the blast in his neck. The horse jerked back, stumbled to the side knocking Vivián down and fell to the ground. The outlaw rose to his knees behind the horse and searched for a target.

REUBEN WATCHED AS THE FOUR MEN TOOK COVER BEHIND the rocks and watched as they looked to the trees. He spotted movement in the trees and moved his Sharps to take in the grassy flat just as one of the outlaws stepped from the trail. The man went to the sorrel, talking to the animal and stroked his neck. He bent down and started to remove the hobbles just as a rifle roared, startling Reuben and the outlaw, but it was easy to see the outlaw had been hit as he dropped to the ground. Reuben watched the man crawl to the rocks and lift his pistol. He was obscured from Reuben's view by a twisted piñon, but Reuben saw and heard as the outlaw returned fire to the posse.

Two pistol shots echoed across the narrow arroyo, and Reuben searched the trees for the second outlaw, but saw nothing. He moved the Sharps back to the grassy flat just in time to see the outlaw rise to his feet and hear what he recognized as a shotgun blast come from the posse. He remembered Julius Sanger carried a shotgun and Reuben watched as the horse took the blast in the neck, dropping the animal to the ground. The outlaw took cover behind the downed horse and fired back at the men in the rocks.

Reuben glanced at the four posse men behind the rocks and saw the man called Carter lifting his rifle and searching for a shot. Reuben knew most men, unless they were the exception and spent a lot of time using firearms, were not very good shots and the longer they kept up this battle, the greater the chance someone would get killed.

Reuben drew a bead on the outlaw, from the corner of his eye he saw Carter move to adjust his shot, and Reuben squeezed the trigger on his Sharps, hearing the rifle of Carter echo the blast. The big rifle roared and bucked, but Reuben knew his sight was true and through the scope, he had one last glimpse of the outlaw as blood blossomed on the man's forehead and he fell backwards into the grass, spooking the black horse who fought his hobbles to get away, crashing into the trees.

Reuben saw Carter jump up and shout, "I got him! I got him!" but Reuben knew it was his shot that finished the outlaw, but he also knew it was not important who killed him and would let Carter take the credit if that was what he wanted. But there was still one more outlaw and Reuben searched the trees and the portion of their camp, but the other man was nowhere to be seen, until he sprang from the trees to see his brother on the ground.

30 / DIVISION

Foley rode beside Billy Youngh, yet sat silent in the
saddle, willing to offer his opinion or counsel only
when asked. Youngh looked at the old timer whose reputation among the prospectors and within the gold fields
was as a man willing to help just about anyone but also
having strong opinions of his own. He was often
referred to as 'an onery cuss' but he was also known to
help anyone that asked. Billy worked up his resolve and
finally asked, "You heard what McCannon did with those
two from Tarryall, what do you think about the
hangin'?"

Foley breathed deep as if readying himself to dive
deep underwater and turned to look at Billy. "Dumbest
thing I ever heard of a man doin' to another."

"But how would you have stopped it?"

"Shot him if I had to, but short of that, I'd have told
him to do it his ownself by his ownself! It's folks like the
bunch that was with him that ain't got no backbone to
stand up for what's right and against what's wrong! And
I ain't talkin' 'bout no 'line in the sand' like some of 'em

do, I'm talkin' 'bout facin' up to them what do wrong and stoppin' it!"

Youngh looked at the older man, and feeling chastised, shook his head and turned to look at the narrow game trail they were following that sided the long ridge west of the arroyo with the outlaws. He looked back at Foley. "What if he, McCannon, tries it again with these two?" nodding to the ridge above them.

"Then we'll stand up agin' it! But I don't reckon we'll hafto do that."

"Why not?"

"That fella I was ridin' with, he's got more sand than anyone I know, an' the onliest reason he come along was to put a stop to that kinda nonsense."

Youngh frowned, glanced back to Foley and then to the trail ahead. "You reckon we're far enough along for us to cross over?"

"I reckon," answered Foley, but the racketing sound of gunfire from the other side of the ridge determined their action for them. Youngh motioned to the others and slid to the ground.

"Let tether our horses here and skedaddle o'er the ridge. Sounds like the fight's already started!"

Foley was already on the ground beside him, rifle in hand as he turned to look through the trees for a path to the top. He started through the thick juniper and piñon making his own trail to the top, suspecting the rest of the posse to be in trouble, he wanted to get there before it was too late. Billy Youngh and the others followed close behind, surprised how the old man was able to readily outdistance them as they struggled for footing on the steep hillside marked with boulders, shale, and whenever there was soil, cactus.

MCCANNON KEPT WELL BEHIND COVER UNTIL CARTER started crowing like a rooster that he had killed the outlaw. With another look around, McCannon slowly lifted his head above cover, glancing from one man to the other, until a figure came from the trees at a run, stopped beside the downed outlaw and looked around for his assailants. McCannon thought he recognized the man and saw his own men grabbing at their rifles or lifting them to shoot and he jumped up, lifting his arms high and shouted, "NO! NO! NO! Don't shoot! That's Billy Youngh!" The lone man turned to face McCannon, glared an evil-eyed stare, snarled, and showed his Jack-O-Lantern grin with big teeth flashing, then ducked away and disappeared into the trees.

"That wasn't Youngh! Why'd you stop us?" asked a frustrated Joseph Lamb, swinging around with his Springfield at his hip and a malevolent glare on his face. His anger flared at the captain, thinking he was showing his cowardice after hiding in the rocks and telling others to do the shooting and now keeping them from shooting the second of the two outlaws.

"But . . . but . . . I thought it was Billy! They were coming from the other side, and I thought it was him. He had a coat just like Billy's!" pleaded the captain.

Reuben had slid and bounded down from his promontory atop the east ridge and trotted into the midst of the argument, glanced at the captain and back at Lamb and Carter. "Hold on, boys! Doesn't Billy have a coat like that fella had? And aren't they 'bout the same size?" asked Reuben, looking at the three men of McCannon's group.

Julius Sanger spoke up, "Yeah, he did, but Billy don't have no black beard like that fella!"

"Then let's get after him!" suggested Reuben, heading

210

to the trail that led to the outlaws' camp. With a glance over his shoulder, he took to the trail, the Sharps hanging by a woven strap at his back, pistol in hand. Sanger and Lamb followed with Carter staying with McCannon to wait for the others. Reuben trotted up the twisting trail, keeping low and looking through the trees for any sign of the fleeing outlaw. He broke from the trees into the camp that appeared to have some things scattered about, but no outlaw. Reuben looked at the edge of the trees, searching for any sign, but found none.

Sanger went to the gear stacked to one side and started rummaging through the stuff. "Hey, lookee here! One o' them fellas was writin' in this here book!" holding the leather-bound journal high above his head.

"What's it say?" asked Lamb as he looked through more of the gear.

"Dunno. I can't read!" answered Sanger, head hanging as he mumbled his reply.

Reuben went to Sanger's side, accepted the journal, and started flipping through the pages. Near the last page he paused, shaking his head. "Says here they killed thirty-two men!"

"Thirty-two?" exclaimed Sanger, "I didn't think it was that many!"

"Me neither," replied Lamb.

Suddenly a pistol blasted from above, the bullet grazing the top of Joseph Lamb's shoulder, prompting him to dive toward the pile of gear for cover. Another shot cut through the tail of Sanger's coat, making him dive behind a tree. Reuben spotted gun smoke at the point of rocks at the edge of the overhang and snapped off a quick shot then another at the edge, but there was no answer. Without a target, Reuben slowly moved from under the overhang, searching the edge of the big rock, pistol held before him, and worked his way to the trees.

A voice came from the trees, "You fellas alright?" It was McCannon, staying behind cover in the trees as he inquired about the men.

"We're alright," replied Reuben. "Lamb was grazed, and Sanger's coat is holier than it was before, but we're alright."

"Did you get the outlaw?"

"Nope. I reckon he's long gone by now. But he is afoot," answered Reuben.

As they spoke, the rest of the posse came through the trees, sounding more like a herd of elk than a bunch of man hunters. Foley stepped into the clearing, looked at Reuben, nodded, then to the others. Sanger was tending to the graze on Lamb's shoulder and Reuben nodded to the pile of gear left behind by the outlaws.

When McCannon came from the trees, Reuben handed off the journal. "You might want to give that a good read, and if it's the truth, these two killed a lot more than we know."

McCannon frowned, glanced at the journal and to the men picking through the gear. He nodded toward Youngh. "See there, his coat is a lot like the outlaw's, and they're 'bout the same size. It's no wonder I mistook him for Youngh."

"I understand," answered Reuben, seeing McCannon for the man he really was, a leader that more willingly sent his men into danger than to risk his own life for others. Reuben shook his head as he took a seat on the grey log nearby. McCannon looked at him. "Don't you think we should take off after the other'n?"

"Through that timber? Not the smartest thing we can do, too easy for him to lay an ambush."

"But we're supposed to take both of 'em in, or hang 'em!" growled the Captain, seeming to regain his bravado.

"Then how 'bout you and me follow him a little way just in case he's layin' up there," nodding to the overhang, "waitin' for us?"

"Uh, uh," stammered the captain, looking at the rest of the men as they sorted through the plunder taken by the killers. He started to raise his hand and call for one of the men but was stopped by Reuben, "No, not them. You and me, c'mon, Captain. Unless I miss my guess, we won't go far, 'sides, there's somethin' else I want to show you."

The captain frowned, glancing around at his men hoping for a reprieve but none came. He looked at Reuben, nodded, "Lead the way, then."

"Never thought any different, Captain," replied Reuben as he hefted his Sharps and started for the trees.

Reuben spotted the faint path the killers had used to get to the top of the overhang, stopped and bent back to look above, then started up the steep line, often using the butt of his Sharps to aid him in his climb. He heard the captain wheezing behind him and sending rocks clattering down the hillside. Before cresting, Reuben stopped, motioned for the captain to stop, and listened. All he heard was the breeze whispering through the pines and the distant scream of a circling bird of prey.

Reuben pushed to the top of the overhang, walked out to the point, and looked down at the others, then turned back to search for the outlaw's trail. He spotted tracks in the dry soil and the crushed blades of bunch grass, a broken branch on an aspen sapling, and other sign farther on, but he stopped and turned to face the captain.

Captain McCannon stopped, looked at Reuben and questioned, "Aren't we going after him?"

"No, Captain, we're not. I'm not, you're not, and the rest of the men are not."

"What do you mean trying to tell me what to do and ordering me and my men about?!" blustered the captain, trying to show his rank and force.

Reuben sat on a nearby rock, leaned his rifle at his side, nodded toward another rock for the captain to be seated. "Now, Captain, we've got one of the pair, we have their horses, and we have all their plunder. All that one escaped with was his pistol and maybe a rifle, and he's got a long way to go to get out of this territory. What your concern should be is for the safety of your men and the people of South Park. Am I right?"

The captain's brow furrowed as he glared at Reuben and nodded without answering.

Reuben asked, "You know a Captain Theodore Dodd?"

"Why yes, I do. It was his outfit that cleaned out that nest, Mace's Hole, of Confederates!"

"Ummhmmm. And did you hear of him doin' anythin' else?"

"Well, yes. His outfit put a stop to the stage robberies, kept the gold shipments out of the Rebels' hands!"

"And if you were to check with Captain Dodd about me and my wife, you might be surprised what you'd find," explained Reuben as he pulled the deputy marshal badge from his pocket and displayed it for the captain.

"You're a deputy marshal?" asked an incredulous McCannon.

"Yes, but as far as the rest of the men, I'm just Reuben Grundy, understand?"

"Uh, yes, but why don't we go after the other outlaw?"

"Because your men are exhausted, you have no provisions, and that outlaw would probably kill several of those men before he would be taken alive. You got one of them, and that journal will tell how many he killed and more besides. Count this a victory and take care of your men and get them back safe and sound. You'll be praised for it and the people of South Park will consider you a hero. Plus, I'll be notifyin' the commander at Fort Garland to be on the lookout for the other man, I believe the journal said his name was Felipe Espinosa, and he'll have somebody in charge of any man hunt in the San Luis Valley, which was the Espinosa's home. Now, isn't that enough?"

"And no one should know about you being a marshal?" he asked.

"That's right. It's just between you and me. The only reason I came on this escapade was to keep you from hangin' any innocents, and now that's over, might as well head home, ya reckon?"

The captain grinned, nodded, and started back to the camp. As he passed, Reuben said, "Foley and I will take a different route, but we'll probably be there before you."

E lly looked every bit the lady with her two-piece dress made of blue flower print cotton. Pleated lace that matched the blue flowers decorated the collar and a matching reticule hung at her side. The hoop skirt drifted over the boardwalk totally obscuring the matching slippers. Her bonnet shaded her face and hair as she walked beside Augusta Tabor on their morning shopping excursion. They stepped into the dining room of the Pacific Hotel and were seated at a table by the window to enjoy the warmth of the morning sun.

As they were seated, Elly loosened the strings on her bonnet and let it fall to her shoulders and back. Augusta did much the same as she seated herself and looked at her friend and charge. "Now, my dear, tell me, what's this I hear about you having some grand adventure on your ride yesterday?" asked Augusta, reaching for her cup of tea and taking a sip as she looked over the rim of her cup at the blue eyes of Elly Grundy.

"Oh, it was nothing really. I wanted to get some fresh air and get out of town, maybe see some of the sights in the goldfield. As I was returning, two men apparently mistook me for one of the women of the row and demanded I accompany them to their cabin. However, I, of course, was not interested and started to ride past them, but one of the men grabbed the reins of my horse and insisted. But I explained to them that what they were doing was against the law, but they did not understand until I explained it further," shared Elly as she also took a sip of her tea.

"But, from what I hear, one of the men was shot; is that true?"

"Well, I suppose it is, but I was simply demonstrating the power of the law."

"But my dear, there is no 'law' in Buckskin outside of the Miner's Court and . . . well, I don't understand." She looked askance at Elly with lifted eyebrows as she leaned closer as if they shared some secret.

Elly smiled. "It wasn't the Miner's Court law that I explained to them, it was Sam's law." Elly dropped her eyes as she reached for the jelly laden crumpet on the platter.

"Sam's law?" asked Augusta.

"Yes, ma'am, Samuel Colt's law, it seems that is the only law that men recognize in these untamed lands."

"You mean the law of a gun?" asked an amazed Augusta. Although she and her husband had been in many mining camps and lawless country, she had always been protected and sheltered by her husband and his grubstaked partners.

"That's correct. Among men of that sort that are accustomed to using their brawn and bluster to have their way, it usually takes a Colt to make them reconsider."

"A gun? You mean you shot him?" asked Augusta, dropping her voice and leaning toward Elly, with glances right and left to see if anyone heard her question. But they were at the table that sat alone in the nook of the bay window.

"Yes, I did."

"But what were you doing with a gun?" whispered Augusta, feeling complicit in some crime or wrongdoing.

"I always carry a pistol and a knife. A woman can't be too careful in places like Buckskin."

"Do you have them now?" whispered Augusta, looking around at the other patrons of the restaurant that were paying no mind to the ladies.

"Why, of course. I'm never without it," replied Elly, smiling at her new friend. "It's in my reticule!" she stated as she nodded to the lady's handbag sitting on the table beside her.

Augusta's eyes flared as she looked at the bag and back at Elly. "Well, I declare!"

Elly smiled as she looked at Augusta. "Aren't these crumpets delicious?"

They finished their tea with the usual small talk of weather, fashions, and the preacher's meetings, and walked together from the restaurant. They walked on the boardwalk on the shady side of the street, making their way to the lady's boutique, when two men stumbled from the alley way, apparently drunk and pushing, and shoving one another and using coarse language. The big man saw the ladies and stood erect, leering at the two until he recognized Elly. "You!" He growled the words, unconsciously putting his good hand on his bandaged elbow as if to protect it from the woman.

"Please excuse us," asked Elly, speaking softly and glancing around at the others on the boardwalk and in the street that stopped and looked at the women and the big brute of a man known as Black Mike with his partner, Nikko. The behavior of the men was contrary to the custom of the day that showed respect to all women, especially to those that were obviously ladies, and the few men in the street and on the boardwalk stopped and watched.

"You did this to me! You had no right! We just wanted a little company!" growled Black Mike as his partner tugged at his shirt, trying to get him away from the women. Any man that showed disrespect or harmed a woman would quickly meet with the vengeance of the male population of the town, regardless of his reasoning.

"C'mon, Mike, let's get outta here! People are watchin'!" pleaded Nikko.

Black Mike jerked away from his partner and raised his good arm as if to strike Elly, but the click of a cocking hammer stopped him. His eyes flared as he looked at the muzzle of the pistol that pointed at his face. Elly said, "Now, apologize!" she demanded, waving the pistol in the direction of her friend, Augusta.

"Uh, uh, . . ." growled the big man, frozen and standing still as a statue, his arm still raised as he muttered, "I'm sorry, ma'am, real sorry. Won't happen again, honest!"

"And me?" added Elly, starting to smile at the man's predicament and embarrassment.

"Uh, yeah, you too. I'm sorry," rumbled the deep bass voice of the big man, glancing from one woman to the other.

"And, Mike, don't ever try that again with any woman!" declared Elly, nodding to the many men that were watching and appeared ready to come to her aid. "I don't think the men of this town would treat you very kindly after this."

"Uh, yes'm. I'm sorry."

Elly motioned with her pistol for the two men to cross the street and get far away from them. Nikko grabbed Black Mike's sleeve and tugged, prompting the frustrated man to heed his friend's prompting, and moved off the boardwalk to cross the dusty street.

Elly chuckled. "Well, that was interesting," glancing at a speechless Augusta, who stood shaking her head as she watched the two men disappear in the crowd of men outside the Three Deuces tavern.

"This is certainly a day I will never forget," declared Augusta, withdrawing a fan from her reticule to cool off. Both women were smiling and laughing as they entered the dressmaker's shop to see two women with wide eyes as they entered. It was obvious the women had seen what happened on the boardwalk and were astounded as the pistol-packing woman entered their store.

"CAPTAIN, WE HAVEN'T HAD ANYTHING TO EAT SINCE DAY 'fore yestiday, an' we're almighty hungry! How 'bout we go on into Cañon City, get us some supplies and rest, then we can come back to Buckskin?" suggested Billy Youngh as he stood beside the captain.

"You're right Billy, that's what we'll do, but first we need to sort through all this plunder and gear those murderers left behind," replied McCannon, motioning to the stack of gear on the far side of the fire. He looked around at the men, noticed Reuben and Foley were missing and asked, "Where's Foley and his partner?"

"They said they were headin' back to Buckskin. Their horses were back at their camp, so they had to hoof it over there. If you want 'em, I can mount up and catch 'em," offered Youngh.

"Nah, Grundy said they were gonna head on back. Let 'em go," replied McCannon. He looked around at the men, several were sorting through the killers' gear and Sanger had stuffed the journal in his belt at his back. "Sanger! Bring me that journal, and Lamb, you an' Sherwood and Fredricks start digging a hole to put that body in!" ordered the captain, motioning to the body of Vivián Espinosa. "We need to get started to Cañon City and get us some grub!"

FOLEY WAS DOWN ON ONE KNEE, HIS HAND BESIDE ONE OF the many tracks that crossed the trail south of Three Mile Mountain, the same mountain where the posse had met up at the previous camp of Foley and Reuben. "What'dya think?" asked Reuben, leaning his elbows on the pommel of his saddle as he leaned over to look at Foley.

"That's gotta be forty or fifty horses, all mounted and prob'ly carryin' scalp huntin' warriors!" answered Foley as he stood. "And comin' from that direction, I guess 'em to be Cheyenne Dog Soldiers. But what bothers me is, are they meetin' up with the Utes to bring war to the settlers and prospectors or are they lookin' for the Utes to wage war. 'Course they could be wantin' to make war against the Ute!" He stood, shook his head, arched his back with his hands at his belt, looked up at Reuben. "Either way, it ain't no good cuz that means blood's gonna be flowin' some'eres."

"Then let's get a move on," stated Reuben as he looked at the sun, "I figger we got five, maybe six hours of daylight, and I'm wantin' to get back to my wife!"

Foley chuckled. "You don't need to be worryin' 'bout her! Ain't no Injuns gonna be goin' agin' that many men

221

such as there be in Buckskin cuz they'd hafta get past Fairplay to do it!"

"Have you ever known Indians to stick to the roads instead of makin' their own way? If they wanna get to Buckskin, there's plenty of ways they can do it and very few of 'em go through Fairplay!" stated Reuben, sitting up in his saddle.

They had been on the trail for four hours before they came to the tracks of the natives, now they started out across South Park, the sun high over their left shoulder and aiming for the mountains on the western horizon. Reuben rode quietly, his hips and legs unconsciously moving with the gait of the long-legged blue roan. The creak of saddle leather, the shuffle of hooves in the heavy dust on the long-dry trail, and the occasional clatter of hooves on rocks served as a lullaby to the tired men, eyes drooping for want of sleep.

The sun stayed true to its arc of time, making its way to the western horizon, stretching shadows eastward, making silhouettes of the saw tooth mountains, and taking its warmth to hide behind the peaks that harbored glaciers and snowpack. As the golden orb cradled itself between the bald mountain tips, it sent lances of gold shooting into the darkening sky. And still they rode, ducking their heads so the hat brims shaded their eyes, eyes that sought refuge behind heavy lids.

Yet tugging at Reuben's heartstrings was the image of his blue-eyed blonde, Elly. He rode to be at her side once again, and he would let nothing, and no one keep him from her. His head bobbed in sleep, jerking him awake to see the brilliant display of God's creation, made perfect in the sunset of this one day.

Reuben and Foley made camp on the Middle Fork of the South Platte River, turning in to their blankets shortly after midnight, stopping only because the horses were pretty well done in and needed the rest. But they were back in the saddle before first light. By staying near the river, the trail was easy, and cover was plentiful with the tall pines that claimed the bottom land that lay in the shadow of the long ridge called Red Hill.

Late morning saw them ride into Fairplay and stop at the hitch rail in front of Molly B's café for some breakfast. As they made quick time over their plates of steak, potatoes, and the rare treat of fresh eggs, they overheard the conversation at the nearby table.

"Doc, I don't think it was the same ones, after all there was murders down to Ute Pass and clear up to Tarryall and Kenosha. I even heard tell of dead bodies found o'er at California Gulch!" emphatically declared an old timer with a tobacco-stained beard that bobbed up and down with every word. His table mate was attired like a businessman with a starched collar, a string tie, and an unstained white muslin shirt, all stuffed behind a tight-fitting linen frock coat and linen trousers.

"But what they say is all those bodies were mutilated in a similar fashion. No, I tend to think like those that believe it's the same killer or killers," replied the man called Doc. "Anymore, it just isn't safe to travel alone!"

Reuben watched Foley whose back was to the talkers and was not surprised at his reaction to the conversation. Foley leaned back in his chair and turned to face the two men, "Pardon me, gentlemen, but I couldn't help but overhear your talk about the killers that have been leavin' mutilated bodies all over South Park."

"Why yes, we have been discussing those killings. Is there something you would like to add?" replied the one referred to as Doc.

Foley turned his chair toward the nearby table and said, "I don't think you need worry 'bout them fellers anymore. One of 'em's been kilt, and the other'n ran off way down south. No sir, I'm purty sure there's no need to fear them no more!"

Both men frowned, looking at one another and then to Foley. The Doc asked, "And how can you be so certain of this?"

"Wal, it were me'n muh partner here whut found 'em, and he kilt one 'fore the other'n ran off afoot through the woods. You see, they was brothers, an' they left behind a journal that said they done kilt thirty-two men!" proudly asserted Foley. "They was Felipe Espinosa and Vivián Espinosa from down San Luis Valley way."

"No, you don't say!" replied a baffled Doc, frowning at Foley and glancing at Reuben who was busy cleaning his plate with a fresh biscuit.

"Yup! Shore 'nuff!" proudly answered Foley. "We was

with the posse that came outta Buckskin, led by Captain McCannon!"

Reuben interrupted when he spoke to Foley, "And if you don't turn around here and finish your breakfast, I'm gonna hafta leave you behind!"

As they put Fairplay behind them and pushed into the valley of the South Platte, bound for Buckskin, Reuben asked, "How'd you know it was me that killed that fella?"

Foley chuckled, grinning. "I know those men in the posse, and ain't a one of 'em a good 'nuff shot to hit a man in the forehead 'ceptin' with a fryin' pan. And I knowed where you was, an' when I looked at the body, I could tell you was in a straight line from yore big rock on that far slope. So, I just figgered it were you!"

"Well, don't go braggin' on it, cuz I'm thinkin' that fella named Carter was convinced he killed him and will prob'ly do a little struttin' around about it. So, let him take the credit, cuz I sure don't want it!"

It was early afternoon when the two rode into Buckskin and Foley looked at Reuben.

"Wal partner, I reckon this is where we split comp'ny. You're stayin' yonder at the hotel and my cabin is farther up the crick. I was just in town the day they gathered up the posse and I joined up. You gonna be around long?"

"I dunno. I'll be talkin' with Elly, that's my wife, about what we'll be doin' the rest of the summer and where we might go explore. We talked about puttin' up a cabin somewhere and Preacher Dyer said there were many abandoned cabins in the goldfields that could be had just for movin' into 'em, but we both kinda like bein' away by ourselves, so . . ."

"Well, I might be back in town tomorry an' I'll stop in at the hotel to see if yore still around. I might know of a couple cabins that might suit'cha."

Reuben grinned, stretched out his hand. "Well, partner. It's been good ridin' with you and if we don't see each other again, always know we'll have you in our prayers!"

"Wal, I for durn shore can use some prayers," replied Foley, shaking Reuben's hand and nodding. As Reuben reined up before the hotel and swung a leg over Blue's rump, Foley tipped his hat and pushed on through town to return to his cabin.

Reuben watched him leave, stepped up on the boardwalk and started to push through the front door of the hotel when a voice behind him said, "Well, it's about time!" and Elly was in his arms as he turned around. Their embrace was almost as long as his absence and while they clung to one another, people crowded past, hardly noticing, all bent on their own lives and loves and most harbored their lust for gold rather than a mate.

When they finally leaned apart, Elly dabbed at tears and laughed as Reuben also wiped away a few tears that had made a path through the dust on his face. She looked up at him, laughed at his weathered face and said, "You need a bath!"

Reuben laughed and answered, "But I have to take care of Blue first, then I'll come back for that bath, and you can catch me up on all the preaching of Preacher Dyer!"

Elly chuckled and cocked her head to the side, a habit she had when she was flirting or trying to avoid recompense for wrongdoing, and said, "Uh, I didn't go to all his meetings, I was lost without you by my side."

IT WAS A FRESHLY SCRUBBED AND ATTIRED REUBEN THAT accompanied the lovely Elly Mae into the dining room of the Pacific Hotel, and the handsome couple turned many heads of the locals. They took the familiar table by the window and Reuben seated Elly, took his own seat, and stretched his arm across the table to grasp Elly's hand. She dropped her eyes in a bashful display of modesty and giggled as she looked back up at her hand-some man. "I really missed you! And I don't want to be left behind again, I don't care if you're with an entire company of cavalry or what have you, I just can't abide being left!" Her words were not harsh but the glint of mischief in her eyes and the firm set of her mouth served as an admonishment to Reuben.

"But it was for your own safety, Elly. That's the only reason I would go anywhere without you," pleaded Reuben, his forehead wrinkling in a bit of a frown.

"And what did you do that was so dangerous that I haven't been through before?"

"Uh, well, half the posse split off and caught a couple men they thought were outlaws and hung 'em, twice!" he started.

"Twice? How can you hang somebody twice?"

"They strung 'em up, let 'em down, and strung 'em up again, and let 'em down again! Or so they tell me."

"You weren't there?"

"No, I was with Foley, he's the one that's goin' to join us for dinner. We were scoutin' to the south, lookin' for sign of the killers."

"And did you find any sign?"

"No, but we ran into a band of Utes under Kaniache and had a little set-to with them, a couple times."

"So, I can fight the Arapaho and the Cheyenne Dog Soldiers, but I can't fight the Ute?" she asked, stubbornly pushing to make her point.

"Well . . ." started Reuben, squirming a little and looking out the window, "Hey, there's Foley!" As the man came into the dining room, he was outfitted in what he called 'Goin' to meetin' duds', linen trousers and jacket over a cotton shirt and a broad smile that greeted everyone he saw. Reuben stood to wave him over to their table and as he neared, he greeted his friend with a handshake, and introduced Elly.

"Ma'am, it's pleased I am to meet'chu. Hope you don't mind my hornin' in on your dinner, but I just had to come to make sure you was real. The way Reuben kept goin' on about'chu, I was beginnin' to think you was just a pigment of his imagination!"

Elly smiled and nodded to the old timer as Reuben corrected him, "I think you mean 'figment' of my imagination."

"That's whut I said, ain't it?"

"You said pigment, that's what they put in paint and such to add color. Figment is a part of something you just imagine to be real."

"Well, whatever it is, you certainly are real, and you are colorful!" added a grinning Foley as he seated himself at the end of the table.

AFTER A SUMPTUOUS MEAL, THE WAITRESS BROUGHT LARGE pieces of hot apple pie and the eyes of the men were almost as big as the whole pie. Both laughed as they glanced to one another, but they wasted no time in finishing the delicious dessert. After Foley finished his off, he pushed back from the table a little, leaned his elbows on the edge of the table and looked from Reuben to Elly and asked, "So, you are wantin' to get to the mountains and away from these crazy goldfields, are ye?"

Reuben nodded, placing his napkin on the table beside the plate, and explained, "We never planned on comin' to the gold fields, it was more of a curiosity for us, but the mountains are where we want to be. I thought we'd find us place to build a cabin, you know, back in the trees, somewhere near a stream and good grass for the animals, and just have some time to ourselves."

"I understand. When we first talked, I thought you might want to take one of the many abandoned cabins up the creek by the gold diggin's, but those places shore ain't purty or scenic and none of 'em's too far away. But you know, I been all over this country and some of the purtiest is down south of here a spell. Back when I was a young pup, I done some trappin' up in the Wet Mountains south of the Arkansas river. It was purty country, but I didn't do much good at trappin'. There used to be a trader down thataway name of Maurice Le Duc, had him a bit of a fort they called Buzzard's Roost. He traded with the Arapaho and the Ute, but the last I heard he'd done packed up and went to Californy. Don't reckon there's nothin' left o' that fort now. But back in those mountains there's plenty of game, good water, and mighty purty country, yessiree."

"How far is that from here?" asked Reuben, leaning forward and putting his arms on the table as he looked at his friend.

"Oh, three, four days, maybe five, dependin' on how big a hurry you get into," chuckled the old man. "And then if you want to see Heaven on earth, I'd go on over them mountains into the big valley below the Sangre de Cristo Mountain range!"

"Sangre de Cristo? That's Blood of Christ isn't it?" asked Elly, showing a bit of a frown.

"Yup, shore 'nuff. 'Bout the purtiest mountain range ya' ever wanna see. It goes from just south of here all the way down almost to that country they be callin' Texas!"

"How did a mountain range get a name like that?"

"Wal, seems there was some o' them black robes, you know, Priests with the Spaniards, had 'em a mission o'er there but they didn't treat the natives too good. So, the Utes rebelled agin' 'em, and when the priests were 'bout to be put to death, they looked at the mountains just as the settin' sun was paintin' 'em red and they called out, "Sangre de Cristo" and the name kinda stuck!"

THREE DAYS BROUGHT THEM SOUTH OUT OF SOUTH PARK and down the Currant Creek Road to Cañon City. They stopped in at Clelland and Peabody General Store and added some building tools to their gear. Foley had volunteered to join them, promising to be more help than a hindrance, thinking mostly about the Utes they might encounter, and he was guiding them into the mountains.

Two more days and they topped out of the Wet Mountains and stopped to take in the panorama of the Sangre de Cristo mountains that stretched from as far as they could see to the west to even farther to the south-east. It was a line of rugged peaks that seemed to march endlessly into the distance like a brigade of blue clad soldiers with white feather plumed hats. The three sat silent to take in the vista of the mountains and the lush green valley that lay at the edge of the black timbered skirts of those mountains. Elly looked at Reuben, smiling, and said, "We're home!"

Reuben chuckled, looking from his bride to his friend. He took in a deep breath, looking around at the scattered trees that dotted the hills where they sat, nodded to a rocky knoll that protruded from thick timber and said, "That looks like a good place to build our cabin."

Elly looked where he pointed, smiling as she looked back at him and said, "Let's build it with big windows and a veranda so we can look at the mountains any time we want!"

Foley had been still as he looked at a scene he knew very well, but appreciated it all the more, and pointed with his chin. "Look yonder," motioning to the wide grassy valley below where a herd of elk grazed, orange and tan calves cavorting around their mothers and a big herd bull standing to the side overlooking his domain.

Reuben grinned, "Couldn't ask for more. Plenty of game, beautiful scenery, wonderful wife, and a good friend. Yup, I reckon the Lord knew exactly what He was doin' when He brought us here."

TAKE A LOOK AT: ESCAPE TO EXILE

STONECROFT SAGA BOOK ONE

AUTHOR OF THE BEST-SELLING BUCKSKIN CHRONICLES SERIES TAKES US ON AN EPIC JOURNEY IN THE NEW STONECROFT SAGA

It started as a brother defending the honor of his only sister, but it led to a bloody duel and a young man of a prominent family lying dead in the dirt...

Gabriel Stonecroft along with his life-long friend, Ezra, the son of the pastor of the African Methodist Episcopal church, at his side, the journey to the far wilderness of the west would begin. One man from prominent social standing, the other with a life of practical experience, are soon joined in life building adventures.

That journey would be fraught with danger, excitement, and adventure as they face bounty hunters, renegade Shawnee and Delaware Indians, and river pirates. The odds are stacked against the two young men that were lacking in worldly wisdom when it came to life on the frontier. But that reservoir of experience would soon be overflowing with first-hand involvement in happenings that even young dreamers could never imagine.

AVAILABLE NOW

ABOUT THE AUTHOR

Born and raised in Colorado into a family of ranchers and cowboys, **B.N. Rundell** is the youngest of seven sons. Juggling bull riding, skiing, and high school, graduation was a launching pad for a hitch in the Army Paratroopers.   After the army, he finished his college education in Springfield, MO, and together with his wife and growing family, entered the ministry as a Baptist preacher.

Together, B.N. and Dawn raised four girls that are now married and have made them proud grandparents. With many years as a successful pastor and educator, he retired from the ministry and followed in the footsteps of his entrepreneurial father and started a successful insurance agency, which is now in the hands of his trusted nephew. He has also been a successful audiobook narrator and has recorded many books for several award-winning authors. Now finally realizing his lifelong dream, B.N. has turned his efforts to writing a variety of books, from children's picture books and young adult adventure books, to the historical fiction and western genres which are his first love.